PARTY TIME IN MUSSOORIE

Ruskin Bond has been writing for over sixty years, and now has over 120 titles in print—novels, collections of short stories, poetry, essays, anthologies and books for children. His first novel, *The Room on the Roof*, received the prestigious John Llewellyn Rhys Prize in 1957. He has also received the Padma Shri (1999), the Padma Bhushan (2014) and two awards from Sahitya Akademi—one for his short stories and another for his writings for children. In 2012, the Delhi government gave him its Lifetime Achievement Award.

Born in 1934, Ruskin Bond grew up in Jamnagar, Shimla, New Delhi and Dehra Dun. Apart from three years in the UK, he has spent all his life in India, and now lives in Mussoorie with his adopted family.

RUSKIN BOND

PARTY TIME IN MUSSOORIE

RUPA

Published by
Rupa Publications India Pvt. Ltd 2016
7/16, Ansari Road, Daryaganj
New Delhi 110002

Sales centres:
Allahabad Bengaluru Chennai
Hyderabad Jaipur Kathmandu
Kolkata Mumbai

ISBN: 978-81-291-4449-2

Fifth impression 2022

10 9 8 7 6 5

Printed at Repro India Limited, India

Contents

Introduction   *vii*

Belting Around Mumbai   1

Monkeys in the Loo   5

Grandpa Fights an Ostrich   12

At the End of the Road   16

Running for Cover   27

Cricket for the Crocodile   35

Party Time in Mussoorie   49

On the Road to Delhi   56

Mukesh Starts a Zoo   63

The Boy Who Broke the Bank   69

The Trouble with Jinns   76

Breakfast Time   81

Be Prepared   85

Simply Living   90

Adventures in Reading   113

The Postman Knocks   122

George and Ranji   127

My Failed Omelettes—and Other Disasters   130

Introduction

My grandmother had a handy collection of aphorisms and proverbs—many of them of her own making—that came in useful in almost every situation. If for instance, my Uncle Ken had once again eaten up all the food put on the table and then some more from the kitchen and larder, she would say, 'Light suppers make long lives', with just a hint of disapproval. Or if my Aunt Mabel was in one of her grumpy moods, she said, 'God gave us our faces, we give ourselves our expressions.' And to me she often said, 'Life may be short, but a smile is only a second's effort.' A smile can immediately make you feel better. It may not be the medicine for much of life's ills, but it surely lessens the pain.

I have tried to follow this suggestion. The time Uncle Ken and I went for a walk and he insisted on going the zigzag way, I did the same. It was fun. But like all things to do with Uncle Ken, it landed us in a situation where we had to make a hasty exit. While we were being chased away by an irate man from his fields and were dashing away, Uncle Ken's hat flew off. Later, when we had stopped panting, I remembered what Granny had said about looking at the funny side of situations and had a good laugh. Unfortunately, I don't think Uncle Ken saw the lighter side at that moment.

It helps to have such an outlook on finding oneself in the oddest of circumstances. Like the time I was in Mumbai and my belt decided to have some fun by first getting entangled with a fellow passenger's luggage and later with the harness of the horse-drawn buggy I was sitting in. After that, I sat quietly at the book festival I had been taken to attend, to keep my belt out of trouble. And it's not just belts that get me into trouble. There was the time I was sharing a taxi to Delhi with a gentleman with a fierce moustache. He was carrying a book written by me with him. When I told him it was my book, he looked offended that I was trying to lay claim on his property. I gave up on the conversation quickly and filed it away for future use in a story. Similarly, finding animals in the house in unexpected places can be funny. But when I found a monkey sitting on the potty in the bathroom at home, I quickly left it alone. What may seem funny to me, may not be so for the monkey if he is interrupted while looking at the newspaper, sitting on the potty.

I have even been accused by some of my younger audience for being too funny. Once a girl asked me disapprovingly why my ghost stories are not scary enough. 'Your ghosts are too funny,' she grumbled. So I tried to write a few scary ghost stories. But I find benign friendly ghosts just as delightful. So I also wrote about my friend Jimmy, who discovered he was a jinn. That meant he could elongate his arms at will. This ensured that he had a starring role to play in the school basketball team. Later, I tried to warn him about using his elongated arms recklessly, but he wouldn't listen to me and ended up in some pain.

Now it's not always I who sees the funny side to everything. Sometimes, given my presence, the people I am visiting or who are hosting me need this sorely. Take, for example, when it's party time in Mussoorie. There are some who would rather that I stayed home, when I offer to sing them a song or two. There was also the time when on the way home from a party where some interestingly magical pakodas had been served, I mistook the circuit judge for an old woman. I politely raised my cap to him but he sailed past with a dignified look. Later I wondered what he would say if I was ever brought up in front of him. Luckily for me, that has not happened yet.

Mostly, I feel I have been able to live this life enjoying its small moments of happiness and been able to laugh when needed. Now if only I was allowed to sing loudly and happily when walking down the Landour Road to Char Dukan. But Gautam thinks I have fallen sick, and dishes are dropped in alarm and the children stop in their tracks. Nothing to do but to grin and bear it, I say!

Ruskin Bond

Belting Around Mumbai

I have lived to see Bombay become Mumbai, Calcutta become Kolkata, and Madras become Chennai. Times change, names change, and if Bond becomes Bonda I won't object. Place-names may alter but people don't, and in Mumbai I found that people were as friendly and good-natured as ever; perhaps even more than when I was last there twenty-five years ago.

On that occasion I had travelled the Doon Express, a slow passenger train that stopped at every small station in at least five states, taking two days and two nights from Dehra Dun to Bombay. It had been a fairly uneventful journey, except for an incident in the small hours when we stopped at Baroda and a hand slipped through my open window, crept under my pillow, found nothing of value except my spectacles, and decided to take them anyway, leaving me to grope half-blind around Bombay until another pair could be made.

Now I carry three pairs of spectacles: one for reading, one for looking at people, and one for looking far out to sea.

On the Kingfisher flight to Mumbai, I used the second pair, as I like looking at people, especially attractive air hostesses. I found they were looking at me too, but that was because I'd caught my belt (my trouser belt, not my seat-belt) in a fellow-passenger's luggage strap and was proceeding to drag both him and his travel-bag down the aisle. We were diplomatically separated by the aforesaid air hostesses who then guided me to my seat without further mishap.

This reminded me of the occasion many years ago when I auditioned for a role in a Tarzan film.

'Who do you wish to play?' asked the casting director. 'Tarzan, of course,' I said.

He gave me a long hard look. 'Can you swing from one tree to another?' he asked.

'Easily,' I said. 'I can even swing from a chandelier.' And I proceeded to do so, wrecking the hall they sat in, in the process. They begged me to stop.

'Thank you, Mr Bond, you have made your point. But we don't think you have the figure for the part of Tarzan. Would you like to take the part of the missionary who is being cooked to a crisp by a bunch of cannibals? Tarzan will come to your rescue.'

I declined the role with dignity.

And now I was in Mumbai, not to audition for a film, but to inaugurate the Rupa Book Festival. For old time's sake, I arrived at the venue in a horse-drawn carriage. Alighting, my recalcitrant belt-buckle got entangled with the horse's harness and I almost dragged the entire contraption into the Bajaj exhibition hall.

However, the evening's entertainment went off without a

hitch. Gulzar read from Ghalib, Tom Alter read from Gulzar, Mandira Bedi read from Nandita Puri, and everyone read madly from each other, and I sat quietly in a corner to keep my belt out of further entanglements.

The next day I was taken on a tour of the city by a *Hindustan Times* journalist and a photographer. They asked me to pose on the steps of the Asiatic Society's Library, an imposing colonial edifice. While I stood there being photographed, a group of teenagers walked past and I overheard one of them remark: 'Yeh naya model hain.'

I took it as a compliment. At least they didn't call me a purana model. Perhaps there's still a chance to get that Tarzan role. If not Tarzan, then his grandfather.

The same journalist and photographer took me to a market where you could buy anything from books to bras. They thrust a thousand-rupee note into my willing hands and told me I could buy anything I liked, while they took pictures.

'Can I keep the money?' I asked.

'No, you have to spend it.'

So I bought two ladies handbags and two pairs of ladies slippers.

'For your girlfriends?' asked the journalist.

'No,' I said, 'for their mothers.'

Back at the festival hall, I was presented with a beautiful sky-blue T-shirt by a charming lady who wishes to remain anonymous. I wore it the next morning when I was leaving Mumbai.

At the airport, one of the Kingfisher staff complimented me on my dress sense; the first time anyone has done so.

'Your blue shirt matches your eyes,' she said.
After that, I shall definitely fly Kingfisher again.

Monkeys in the Loo

I am fairly tolerant about these monkeys doing the bhangra on my roof, but I do resent it when they start invading my rooms. Not so long ago, I opened the bathroom door to find a very large Rhesus monkey sitting on the potty. He wasn't actually using the potty—monkeys prefer parapet walls—but he had obviously found it a comfortable place to sit, and he showed no signs of vacating the throne when politely requested to do so. Bullies seldom do. So I had to give him a fright by slamming the door as loudly as I could, and he took off through the open window and found his cousins on the hillside.

On another occasion, a female of the species sat on my desk, lifted the telephone receiver and appeared to be making an STD call to some distant relative. Some ladies are apt to linger long over their calls, and I hated to interrupt, but I was anxious to get in touch with my publisher, who took priority; so I pushed her off my desk with a feather-duster. She was so resentful of this intrusion that she made off with my telephone directory and tore it to shreds, scattering pages along the road. As this was something that I had wanted to do for a long time, I could not help admiring her audacity.

The kitchen area of our flat is closely guarded, as I resent sharing my breakfast with creatures great and small. But the other day a wily crow flew in and made off with my boiled egg. I know crows are fond of eggs—other birds' eggs that is—but I did not know that they like them boiled. Anyway, this egg was still piping hot, and the crow had to drop it on the road, where it was seized upon by one of the stray dogs who police this end of the road.

Barking furiously, the dogs run after the monkeys, who simply leap onto the nearest tree or rooftop and proceed to throw insults at the frustrated pack. The dogs never succeed in catching anything except their own kind. Canine intruders from another area are readily attacked and driven away.

Having dressed, breakfasted and written the morning's two or three pages (early morning is the best time to do this), I am free to walk up the road to the bank or post office or tea shop at the top of the hill. If it's springtime, I shall look out for wild flowers. If it's monsoon time; I shall look out for leeches.

Well, it's monsoon time, and we haven't seen the sun for a couple of weeks. Clouds envelop the hills, and a light shower is falling. I have unfurled my bright yellow umbrella, as a gesture of defiance. At least it provides some contrast to the grey sky and the dark green of the hillside. You cannot see the snows or even the next mountain.

There's no one else on the road today, only a few intrepid tourists from Amritsar. I overhead one robust Punjabi complain to his guide: 'You've brought us all the way to the top of this forsaken mountain, and what have you shown us? The kabristan!'

True, the old British graves are all that one can see through the fog. Some of the tombstones have been standing there for close on two centuries. The old abandoned parsonage next door to the cemetery is now the home of Victor Banerjee, the celebrated actor. He enjoys living next door to the graveyard, and one night he defied me to walk home alone past the graves. I am not a superstitious person but I did feel rather uneasy as those old graves loomed up through the mist. I was startled by the cry of a night-bird emanating from behind one of the tombstones. Then a weird, blood-chilling cry rose from a clump of bushes. It was Victor, trying to frighten me—or possibly practising for his next role as Dracula. I was about to break into a run when a large dog—one of our strays—appeared beside me and accompanied me home. On a dark and scary night, even a half-starved mongrel is welcome company. By day, the road holds no terrors. But there are other hazards. On the road near Char Dukan, several small boys are kicking a football around. The ball rolls temptingly towards me. Remembering my football skills of fifty or more years ago, I cannot resist the temptation to put boot to ball. I give it a mighty kick. The ball sails away, the children applaud, I am left hopping about on the road in agony, I had quite forgotten my gout! I'm glad I stuck to writing instead of taking up professional football. At seventy I can still write without inflicting damage on myself.

When I am feeling good, and have the road to myself, I do occasionally break into song. This is the only opportunity I have to sing. Otherwise my musical abilities turn friends into foes.

I am not permitted to sing in the homes of my friends. If I am being driven about in their cars, I am told to remain silent unless we veer off the road or hit an oncoming vehicle. Even at home, the sound of my music causes the girls to drop dishes and the children to find an excuse to stop doing their homework.

'Dada is ill again,' says Gautam, when all I am trying to do is emulate Caruso singing 'Che Gelida Nlanina' (Your Tiny Hand is Frozen) from *La Boheme*. Our tiny hands do freeze up here in the winter, and there's nothing like an operatic aria to get the blood circulating freely. Of course Caruso was a tenor, but I can also sing baritone like Domingo or Nelson Eddy and bass like Chaliapin the great Russian singer. Sometimes I combine all three voices—tenor, baritone, bassand—that's when the window glass shatters and cars come to a screeching halt.

It was a boyhood ambition to be an opera star, but I'm afraid I never made it beyond the school choir. Our music teacher did not appreciate the wide range of my voice. 'Too loud!' she would screech. 'Too flat!'

'Caruso sings in A-flat,' I replied.

'You sound like a warbling frog,' she snapped. 'And you look like one,' I responded.

And that was the end of my brief appearance in cassock and surplice.

But when I'm on the open road—especially when it's raining and I have the road to myself—I am free to sing as loud and as flat as I like, and if flat tyres on passing cars are the result, it's the fault of the tyres and not my singing.

So here we go:

> When you are down and out,
> Lift up your head and shout—
> It's going to be a great day!

There's nothing like a spirited song to raise the flagging spirit. Whenever I feel down and out-and that's often enough—I recall some old favourite and share it with the trees, the birds, and even those pesky monkeys.

> Just like a sunflower
> After a summer shower
> My inspiration is you!

Sloppy, sentimental stuff, but it works.

And there's always the likelihood of a little romance around the corner.

> Some enchanted evening
> You will see a stranger
> Across a crowded room...

Actually, I prefer the winding road to a crowded room. Romantic encounters are more likely when there are not too many people around. Such as the other day, when I had unfurled my new umbrella and was sauntering up the road, singing my favourite rain song, Sinking in the Rain.

I had gone some distance when I noticed a young lady struggling up the road a little way ahead of me. My glasses were wet and misty, but I was determined to share my umbrella with any damsel in distress. So, huffing and puffing, I caught up with her.

'Do share my umbrella,' I offered.

No, she wasn't sweet twenty-one, as I'd hoped. She was nearer eighty. But she was munching on a bhutta, so her teeth were in good order. She took the umbrella from me and munched on ahead, leaving me to get drenched. A retired headmistress, as I discovered later!

She returned the umbrella when we got to Char Dukan, but in future I shall make a frontal approach before making any gallant overtures on the road. Those crowded rooms are safer.

Monsoon time, and umbrellas are taken out and frequently lost. I lost three last year. One was borrowed, and as you know, borrowed books and umbrellas are seldom returned. By some mysterious process they become the permanent property of the borrower. Another disappeared while I was cashing a cheque in the bank. And the third was wrecked in the following fashion.

Coming down from Char Dukan, I found two hefty boys engaged in furious combat in the middle of the road. One was a kick-boxer, the other a kung-fu exponent. Afraid that one of them would be badly hurt, I decided to intervene, and called out, 'Come on boys, break it up!' I thrust my umbrella between them in a bid to end the fracas. My umbrella received a mighty kick, and went sailing across the road and over the parapet. The boys stopped fighting in order to laugh at my discomfiture. One of them retrieved my umbrella, minus its handle.

In a way, I'd been successful as a peacemaker—certainly more successful than the United Nations—although at some cost to my personal property. Well, we peacemakers must be prepared to put up with a little inconvenience.

I'm a great believer in the Law of Compensation (as propounded by Emerson in his famous essay)—that what we do, good or bad, is returned in full measure in this life rather than in the hereafter.

Not long after the incident just described, there was my old friend Vipin Buckshey standing on the threshold with a seasonal gift—a beautiful blue umbrella!

He did not know about the street-fighter, but had read my story 'The Blue Umbrella'—a simple tale about greed being overcome by generosity—and had bought me a blue umbrella in appreciation. I shall be careful not to lose it.

Grandpa Fights an Ostrich

Before my grandfather joined the Indian Railways, he worked for a few years on the East African Railways, and it was during that period that he had his now famous encounter with the ostrich. My childhood was frequently enlivened by this oft-told tale of his, and I give it here in his own words—or as well as I can remember them!

While engaged in the laying of a new railway line, I had a miraculous escape from an awful death. I lived in a small township, but my work lay some twelve miles away, and I had to go to the work-site and back on horseback.

One day, my horse had a slight accident, so I decided to do the journey on foot, being a great walker in those days. I also knew of a short-cut through the hills that would save me about six miles.

This short-cut went through an ostrich farm—or 'camp', as it was called. It was the breeding season. I was fairly familiar with the ways of ostriches, and knew that male birds were very aggressive in the breeding season, ready to attack on the slightest provocation, but I also knew that my dog would scare away any bird that might try to attack me. Strange though it may seem, even the biggest ostrich (and some of them grow to a height of nine feet) will run faster than a racehorse at the sight of even a small dog. So, I felt quite safe in the company of my dog, a mongrel who had adopted me some two months previously.

On arrival at the camp, I climbed through the wire fencing and, keeping a good look-out, dodged across the open spaces between the thorn bushes. Now and then I caught a glimpse of the birds feeding some distance away.

I had gone about half a mile from the fencing when up started a hare. In an instant my dog gave chase. I tried calling him back, even though I knew it was hopeless. Chasing hares was that dog's passion.

I don't know whether it was the dog's bark or my own shouting, but what I was most anxious to avoid immediately happened. The ostriches were startled and began darting to and fro. Suddenly, I saw a big male bird emerge from a thicket about a hundred yards away. He stood still and stared at me for a few moments. I stared back. Then, expanding his short wings and with his tail erect, he came bounding towards me.

As I had nothing, not even a stick, with which to defend myself, I turned and ran towards the fence. But it was an unequal race. What were my steps of two or three feet against the creature's great strides of sixteen to twenty feet? There was only one hope: to get behind a large bush and try to elude the bird until help came. A dodging game was my only chance.

And so, I rushed for the nearest clump of thorn bushes and waited for my pursuer. The great bird wasted no time—he was immediately upon me.

Then the strangest encounter took place. I dodged this way and that, taking great care not to get directly in front of the ostrich's deadly kick. Ostriches kick forward, and with such terrific force that if you were struck, their huge chisel-like nails would cause you much damage.

I was breathless, and really quite helpless, calling wildly for help as I circled the thorn bush. My strength was ebbing. How much longer could I keep going? I was ready to drop from exhaustion.

As if aware of my condition, the infuriated bird suddenly doubled back on his course and charged straight at me. With a desperate effort I managed to step to one side. I don't know how, but I found myself holding on to one of the creature's wings, quite close to its body.

It was now the ostrich's turn to be frightened. He began to turn, or rather waltz, moving round and round so quickly that my feet were soon swinging out from his body, almost horizontally! All the while the ostrich kept opening and shutting his beak with loud snaps.

Imagine my situation as I clung desperately to the wing of the enraged bird. He was whirling me round and round as though he were a discus-thrower—and I the discus! My arms soon began to ache with the strain, and the swift and continuous circling was making me dizzy. But I knew that if I relaxed my hold, even for a second, a terrible fate awaited me.

Round and round we went in a great circle. It seemed as if that spiteful bird would never tire. And, I knew I could not hold on much longer. Suddenly the ostrich went into reverse! This unexpected move made me lose my hold and sent me sprawling to the ground. I landed in a heap near the thorn bush and in an instant, before I even had time to realise what had happened, the big bird was upon me. I thought the end had come. Instinctively I raised my hands to protect my face. But the ostrich did not strike.

I moved my hands from my face and there stood the creature with one foot raised, ready to deliver a deadly kick! I couldn't move. Was the bird going to play cat-and-mouse with me, and prolong the agony?

As I watched, frightened and fascinated, the ostrich turned his head sharply to the left. A second later he jumped back, turned, and made off as fast as he could go. Dazed, I wondered what had happened to make him beat so unexpected a retreat.

I soon found out. To my great joy, I heard the bark of my truant dog, and the next moment he was jumping around me, licking my face and hands. Needless to say, I returned his caresses most affectionately! And, I took good care to see that he did not leave my side until we were well clear of that ostrich camp.

At the End of the Road

Choose your companions carefully when you are walking in the hills. If you are accompanied by the wrong person—by which I mean someone who is temperamentally very different to you—that long hike you've been dreaming of could well turn into a nightmare.

This has happened to me more than once. The first time, many years ago, when I accompanied a businessman-friend to the Pindari Glacier in Kumaon. He was in such a hurry to get back to his executive's desk in Delhi that he set off for the Glacier as though he had a train to catch, refusing to spend any time admiring the views, looking for birds or animals, or greeting the local inhabitants. By the time we had left the last dak bungalow at Phurkia, I was ready to push him over a cliff. He probably felt the same way about me.

On our way down, we met a party of Delhi University boys who were on the same trek. They were doing it in a leisurely, good-humoured fashion. They were very friendly and asked me to join them. On an impulse, I bid farewell to my previous companion—who was only too glad to dash off downhill to where his car was parked at Kapkote—while I made a second ascent to the Glacier, this time in better company.

Unfortunately, my previous companion had been the one with the funds. My new friends fed me on the way back, and in Naini Tal I pawned my watch so that I could have enough for the bus ride back to Delhi. Lesson Two: always carry enough money with you; don't depend on a wealthy friend!

Of course, it's hard to know who will be a 'good companion' until you have actually hit the road together. Sharing a meal or having a couple of drinks together is not the same as tramping along on a dusty road with the water bottle down to its last drop. You can't tell until you have spent a night in the rain, or lost the way in the mountains, or finished all the food, whether both of you have stout hearts and a readiness for the unknown.

I like walking alone, but a good companion is well worth finding. He will add to the experience. 'Give me a companion of my way, be it only to mention how the shadows lengthen as the sun declines,' wrote Hazlitt.

Pratap was one such companion. He had invited me to spend a fortnight with him in his village above the Nayar river in Pauri-Garhwal. In those days, there was no motor-road beyond Lansdowne and one had to walk some thirty miles to get to the village.

But first, one had to get to Lansdowne. This involved getting into a train at Dehra Dun, getting out at Luxor (across the Ganga), getting into another train, and then getting out again at Najibabad and waiting for a bus to take one through the

Tarai to Kotdwara.

Najibabad must have been one of the least inspiring places on earth. Hot, dusty, apparently lifeless. We spent two hours at the bus-stand, in the company of several donkeys, also quartered there. We were told that the area had once been the favourite hunting ground of a notorious dacoit, Sultana Daku, whose fortress overlooked the barren plain. I could understand him taking up dacoity—what else was there to do in such a place—and presumed that he looked elsewhere for his loot, for in Nazibabad there was nothing worth taking. In due course he was betrayed and hanged by the British, when they should instead have given him an OBE for stirring up the sleepy countryside.

There was a short branch line from Nazibabad to Kotdwara, but the train wasn't leaving that day, as the engine driver was unaccountably missing. The bus-driver seemed to be missing too, but he did eventually turn up, a little worse for some late night drinking. I could sympathize with him. If in 1940, Nazibabad drove you to dacoity, in 1960 it drove you to drink.

Kotdwara, a steamy little town in the foothills, was equally depressing. It seemed to lack any sort of character. Here we changed buses, and moved into higher regions, and the higher we went, the nicer the surroundings; by the time we reached Lansdowne, at six thousand feet, we were in good spirits.

The small hill station was a recruiting centre for the Garhwal Rifles (and still is), and did not cater to tourists. There were no hotels, just a couple of tea-stalls where a meal of dal and rice could be obtained. I believe it is much the same forty years on. Pratap had a friend who was the caretaker of an old, little used church, and he bedded us down in the vestry. Early next morning we set out on our long walk to Pratap's village.

I have covered longer distances on foot, but not all in one day. Thirty miles of trudging up hill and down and up again, most of it along a footpath that traversed bare hillsides where the hot May sun beat down relentlessly. Here and there we found a little shade and a freshet of spring water, which kept us going; but we had neglected to bring food with us apart from a couple of rock-hard buns probably dating back to colonial times, which we had picked up in Lansdowne. We were lucky to meet a farmer who gave us some onions and accompanied us part of the way.

Onions for lunch? Nothing better when you're famished. In the West they say, 'Never talk to strangers.' In the East they say, 'Always talk to strangers.' It was this stranger who gave us sustenance on the road, just as strangers had given me company on the way to the Pindar Glacier. On the open road there are no strangers. You share the same sky, the same mountain, the same sunshine and shade. On the open road we are all brothers.

The stranger went his way, and we went ours. 'Just a few more bends,' according to Pratap, always encouraging to the novice plainsman. But I was to be a hillman by the time we returned to Dehra! Hundreds of 'just a few more bends', before we reached the village, and I kept myself going with my off-key rendering of the old Harry Lauder song—

Keep right on to the end of the road,
Keep right on to the end.
If your way be long, let your heart be strong,
So keep right on round the bend.

By the time we'd done the last bend, I had a good idea of how the expression 'going round the bend' had came into existence. A maddened climber, such as I, had to negotiate one bend too many...

But Pratap was the right sort of companion. He adjusted his pace to suit mine; never lost patience; kept telling me I was a great walker. We arrived at the village just as night fell, and there was his mother waiting for us with a tumbler of milk.

Milk! I'd always hated the stuff (and still do) but that day I was grateful for it and drank two glasses. Fortunately it was cold. There was plenty of milk for me to drink during my two-week stay in the village, as Pratap's family possessed at least three productive cows. The milk was supplemented by thick rotis, made from grounded maize, seasonal vegetables, rice, and a species of lentil peculiar to the area and very difficult to digest. Health-food friends would have approved of this fare, but it did not agree with me, and I found myself constipated most of the time. Still, better to be constipated than to be in free flow.

The point I am making is that it is always wise to carry your own food on a long hike or treks in the hills. Not that I could have done so, as Pratap's guest; he would have taken it as an insult. By the time I got back to Dehra—after another exhausted trek, and more complicated bus and train journeys—I felt quite famished and out of sorts. I bought some eggs and bacon rashers from the grocery store across the road from Astley Hall, and made myself a scrumptious breakfast. I am not much of a cook, but I can fry an egg and get the bacon nice and crisp. My needs are simple really. To each his own!

On another trek, from Mussoorie to Chamba (before the

motor-road came into existence) I put two tins of sardines into my knapsack but forgot to take along a can-opener. Three days later I was back in Dehra, looking very thin indeed, and with my sardine tins still intact. That night I ate the contents of both tins.

Reading an account of the same trek undertaken by John Lang about a hundred years earlier, I was awestruck by his description of the supplies that he and his friends took with them.

Here he is, writing in Charles Dickens' magazine, *Household Words*, in the issue of 30 January 1858:

> In front of the club-house our marching establishment had collected, and the one hundred and fifty coolies were laden with the baggage and stores. There were tents, camp tables, chairs, beds, bedding, boxes of every kind, dozens of cases of wine-port, sherry and claret-beer, ducks, fowls, geese, guns, umbrellas, great coats and the like.

He then goes on to talk of lobsters, oysters and preserved soups.

I doubt if I would have got very far on such fare. I took the same road in October 1958, a century later; on my own and without provisions except for the afore-mentioned sardine tins. By dusk I had reached the village of Kaddukhal, where the local shopkeeper put me up for the night.

I slept on the floor, on a sheepskin infested by fleas. They were all over me as soon as I lay down, and I found it impossible to sleep. I fled the shop before dawn.

'Don't go out before daylight,' warned my host. 'There are bears around.'

But I would sooner have faced a bear than that onslaught from the denizens of the sheepskin. And I reached Chamba in time for an early morning cup of tea.

∽

Most Himalayan villages lie in the valleys, where there are small streams, some farmland, and protection from the biting winds that come through the mountain passes. The houses are usually made of large stones, and have sloping slate roofs so the heavy monsoon rain can run off easily. During the sunny autumn months, the roofs are often covered with pumpkins, left there to ripen in the sun.

One October night, when I was sleeping at a friend's house just off the Tehri road, I was awakened by a rumbling and thumping on the roof. I woke my friend Jai and asked him what was happening.

'It's only a bear,' he said.

'Is it trying to get in?'

'No. It's after the pumpkins.'

A little later, when we looked out of a window, we saw a black bear making off through a field, leaving a trail of half-eaten pumpkins.

In winter, when snow covers the higher ranges, the Himalayan bears descend to lower altitudes in search of food. Sometimes they forage in fields. And because they are shortsighted and suspicious of anything that moves, they can be dangerous. But, like most wild animals, they avoid humans as much as possible.

Village folk always advise me to run downhill if chased by

a bear. They say bears find it easier to run uphill than down. I have yet to be chased by a bear, and will happily skip the experience. But I have seen a few of these mountain bears and they are always fascinating to watch.

Himalayan bears enjoy corn, pumpkins, plums, and apricots. Once, while I was sitting in an oak tree on Pari Tibba, hoping to see a pair of pine-martens that lived nearby, I heard the whining grumble of a bear, and presently a small bear ambled into the clearing beneath the tree.

He was little more than a cub, and I was not alarmed. I sat very still, waiting to see what the bear would do.

He put his nose to the ground and sniffed his way along until he came to a large anthill. Here he began huffing and puffing, blowing rapidly in and out of his nostrils so that the dust from the anthill flew in all directions. But the anthill had been deserted, and so, grumbling, the bear made his way up a nearby plum tree. Soon he was perched high in the branches. It was then that he saw me.

The bear at once scrambled several feet higher up the tree and lay flat on a branch. Since it wasn't a very big branch, there was a lot of bear showing on either side. He tucked his head behind another branch. He could no longer see me, so he apparently was satisfied that he was hidden, although he couldn't help grumbling.

Like all bears, this one was full of curiosity. So, slowly, inch by inch, his black snout appeared over the edge of the branch. As soon as he saw me, he drew his head back and hid his face.

He did this several times. I waited until he wasn't looking, then moved some way down my tree. When the bear looked over and saw that I was missing, he was so pleased that he stretched right across to another branch and helped himself to a plum. At that, I couldn't help bursting into laughter.

The startled young bear tumbled out of the tree, dropped through the branches some fifteen feet, and landed with a thump in a pile of dried leaves. He was unhurt, but fled from the clearing, grunting and squealing all the way.

Another time, my friend Jai told me that a bear had been active in his cornfield. We took up a post at night in an old cattle shed, which gave a clear view of the moonlit field.

A little after midnight, the bear came down to the edge of the field. She seemed to sense that we had been about. She was hungry, however. So, after standing on her hind legs and peering around to make sure the field was empty, she came cautiously out of the forest.

The bear's attention was soon distracted by some Tibetan prayer flags, which had been strung between two trees. She gave a grunt of disapproval and began to back away, but the fluttering of the flags was a puzzle that she wanted to solve. So she stopped and watched them.

Soon the bear advanced to within a few feet of the flags, examining them from various angles. Then, seeing that they posed no danger, she went right up to the flags and pulled them down. Grunting with apparent satisfaction, she moved into the field of corn.

Jai had decided that he didn't want to lose any more of his crop, so he started shouting. His children woke up and soon came running from the house, banging on empty kerosene tins.

Deprived of her dinner, the bear made off in a bad temper.

She ran downhill at a good speed, and I was glad that I was not in her way.

Uphill or downhill, an angry bear is best given a very wide path.

∽

Sleeping out, under the stars, is a very romantic conception. 'Stones thy pillow, earth thy bed,' goes an old hymn, but a rolled-up towel or shirt will make a more comfortable pillow Do not settle down to sleep on sloping ground, as I did once when I was a Boy Scout during my prep school days. We had camped at Tara Devi, on the outskirts of Shimla, and as it was a warm night I decided to sleep outside our tent. In the middle of the night I began to roll. Once you start rolling on a steep hillside, you don't stop. Had it not been for a thorny dog-rose bush, which halted my descent, I might well have rolled over the edge of a precipice.

I had a wonderful night once, sleeping on the sand on the banks of the Ganga above Rishikesh. It was a balmy night, with just a faint breeze blowing across the river, and as I lay there looking up at the stars, the lines of a poem by R.L. Stevenson kept running through my head:

Give to me the life I love,
Let the lave go by me,
Give the jolly heaven above
And the byway nigh me.
Bed in the bush with stars to see,
Bread I dip in the river—

There's the life for a man like me,
There's the life for ever.

The following night I tried to repeat the experience, but the jolly heaven above opened up in the early hours, the rain came pelting down, and I had to run for shelter to the nearest Ashram. Never take Mother Nature for granted!

The best kind of walk, and this applies to the plains as well as to the hills, is the one in which you have no particular destination when you set out.

'Where are you off?' asked a friend of mine the other day, when he met me on the road.

'Honestly, I have no idea,' I said, and I was telling the truth.

I did end up in Happy Valley, where I met an old friend whom I hadn't seen for years. When we were boys, his mother used to tell us stories about the bhoots that haunted her village near Mathura. We reminisced and then went our different ways. I took the road to Hathipaon and met a schoolgirl who covered ten miles every day on her way to and from her school. So there were still people who used their legs, though out of necessity rather than choice.

Anyway, she gave me a story to write and thus I ended the day with two stories, one a memoir and the other based on a fresh encounter. And all because I had set out without a plan. The adventure is not in getting somewhere, it's the on-the-way experience. It is not the expected; it's the surprise. Not the fulfilment of prophecy, but the providence of something better than that prophesied.

Running for Cover

The right to privacy is a fine concept and might actually work in the West, but in Eastern lands it is purely notional. If I want to be left alone, I have to be a shameless liar-pretend that I am out of town or, if that doesn't work, announce that I have measles, mumps or some new variety of Asian flu.

Now I happen to like people and I like meeting people from all walks of life. If this were not the case, I would have nothing to write about. But I don't like too many people all at once. They tend to get in the way. And if they arrive without warning, banging on my door while I am in the middle of composing a poem or writing a story, or simply enjoying my afternoon siesta, I am inclined to be snappy or unwelcoming. Occasionally I have even turned people away.

As I get older, that afternoon siesta becomes more of a necessity and less of an indulgence. But it's strange how people love to call on me between two and four in the afternoon. I suppose it's the time of day when they have nothing to do.

'How do we get through the afternoon?' one of them will say.

'I know! Let's go and see old Ruskin. He's sure to entertain us with some stimulating conversation, if nothing else.' Stimulating conversation in mid-afternoon? Even Socrates would have balked at it.

'I'm sorry I can't see you today,' I mutter. 'I don't feel at all well.' (In fact, extremely unwell at the prospect of several strangers gaping at me for at least half-an-hour.)

'Not well? We're so sorry. My wife here is a homeopath.'

It's amazing the number of homeopaths who turn up at my door. Unfortunately they never seem to have their little powders on them, those miracle cures for everything from headaches to hernias.

The other day a family burst in—uninvited of course. The husband was an ayurvedic physician, the wife was a homeopath (naturally), the eldest boy a medical student at an allopathic medical college.

'What do you do when one of you falls ill?' I asked, 'Do you try all three systems of medicine?'

'It depends on the ailment,' said the young man. 'But we seldom fall ill. My sister here is a yoga expert.'

His sister, a hefty girl in her late twenties (still single) looked more like an all-in wrestler than a supple yoga practitioner. She looked at my tummy. She could see I was in bad shape.

'I could teach you some exercises,' she said. 'But you'd have to come to Ludhiana.'

I felt grateful that Ludhiana was a six-hour drive from Mussoorie.

'I'll drop in some day,' I said. 'In fact, I'll come and take a course.'

We parted on excellent terms. But it doesn't always turn out that way.

There was this woman, very persistent, in fact downright rude, who wouldn't go away even when I told her I had bird-flu.

'I have to see you,' she said, 'I've written a novel, and I want you to recommend it for a Booker Prize.'

'I'm afraid I have no influence there,' I pleaded. 'I'm completely unknown in Britain.'

'Then how about the Nobel Prize?'

I thought about that for a minute. 'Only in the science field,' I said. 'If it's something to do with genes or stem cells?'

She looked at me as though I was some kind of worm. 'You are not very helpful,' she said.

'Well, let me read your book.'

'I haven't written it yet.'

'Well, why not come back when it's finished? Give yourself a year—two years—these things should never be done in a hurry.' I guided her to the gate and encouraged her down the steps.

'You are very rude,' she said. 'You did not even ask me in. I'll report you to Khushwant Singh. He's a friend of mine. He'll put you in his column.'

'If Khushwant Singh is your friend,' I said, 'why are you bothering with me? He knows all the Nobel and Booker Prize people. All the important people, in fact.'

I did not see her again, but she got my phone number from someone, and now she rings me once a week to tell me her book is coming along fine. Any day now, she's going to turn up with the manuscript.

Casual visitors who bring me their books or manuscripts are the ones I dread most. They ask me for an opinion, and if I give them a frank assessment they resent it. It's unwise to tell a would-be writer that his memoirs or novel or collected verse would be better off unpublished. Murders have been committed for less. So I play safe and say, 'Very promising. Carry on writing.' But this is fatal. Almost immediately I am asked to write a foreword or introduction, together with a letter of recommendation to my publisher—or any publisher of standing. Unwillingly I become a literacy agent; unpaid of course.

I am all for encouraging the arts and literature, but I do think writers should seek out their own publishers and write their own introductions.

The perils of doing this sort of thing was illustrated when I was prevailed upon to write a short introduction to a book about a dreaded man-eater who had taken a liking to the flesh of the good people of Dogadda, near Lansdowne. The author of the book could hardly write a decent sentence, but he managed to string together a lengthy account of the leopard's depradations. He was so persistent, calling on me or ringing me up that I finally did the introduction. He then wanted me to edit or touch up his manuscript; but this I refused to do. 1 would starve if I had to sit down and rewrite other people's books. But he prevailed upon me to give him a photograph.

Months later, the book appeared, printed privately of course. And there was my photograph, and a photograph of the dead leopard after it had been hunted down. But the local printer had got the captions mixed up. The dead animal's picture earned the line: 'Well-known author Ruskin Bond.' My picture carried the legend: 'Dreaded man-eater, shot after it had killed its 26th victim.'

The printer's devil had turned me into a serial killer.

Now you know why I'm wary of writing introductions.

'Vanity' publishers thrive on writers who are desperate to see their work in print. They will print and deliver a book at your doorstep and then leave you with the task of selling it; or to be more accurate, disposing of it.

One of my neighbours, Mrs Santra—may her soul rest in peace—paid a publisher forty-thousand rupees to bring out a fancy edition of her late husband's memoirs. During his lifetime he'd been unable to get it published, but before he died he got his wife to promise that she'd publish it for him. This she did, and the publisher duly delivered 500 copies to the good lady. She gave a few copies to friends, and then passed away, leaving the books behind. Her heir is now saddled with 450 hardbound volumes of unsaleable memoirs.

I have always believed that if a writer is any good he will find a publisher who will print, bind, and sell his books, and even give him a royalty for his efforts. A writer who pays to get published is inviting disappointment and heartbreak.

Many people are under the impression that I live in splendour in a large mansion, surrounded by secretaries and servants. They are disappointed to find that I live in a tiny bedroom-cum-study and that my living-room is so full of books that there is hardly space for more than three or four visitors at a time.

Sometimes thirty to forty schoolchildren turn up, wanting

to see me. I don't turn away children, if I can help it. But if they come in large numbers I have to meet and talk to them on the road, which is inconvenient for everyone.

If I had the means, would I live in a splendid mansion in the more affluent parts of Mussoorie, with a film star or TV personality as my neighbour? I rather doubt it. All my life I've been living in one or two rooms and I don't think I could manage a bigger establishment. True, my extended family takes up another two rooms, but they see to it that my working space is not violated. And if I am hard at work (or fast asleep) they will try to protect me from unheralded or unwelcome visitors.

And I have learnt to tell lies. Especially when I'm asked to attend school functions as a chief guest or in some formal capacity. To spend two or three hours listening to speeches (and then being expected to give one) is my idea of hell. It's hell for the students and it's hell for me. The speeches are usually followed (or preceded) by folk dances, musical interludes or class plays, and this only adds to the torment. Sports days are just as bad. You can skip the speeches (hopefully), but you must sit out in the hot sun for the greater part of the day, while a loudspeaker informs you that little Parshottam has just broken the school record for the under-nine high jump, or that Pamela Highjinks has won the hurdles for the third year running. You don't get to see the events because you are kept busy making polite conversation with the other guests. The only occasion when a sports' event really came to life was when a misdirected discus narrowly missed decapitating the headmaster's wife.

Former athletes and sportsmen seldom visit me. They have difficulty making it up my steps. Most of them have problems with their knees before they are fifty. They hobble (for want of a better word). Once their playing days are over, they start hobbling. Nandu, a former tennis champion, can't make it up my steps, nor can Chand—a former wrestler. Too much physical activity when young has resulted in an early breakdown of the body's machinery. As Nandu says, 'Body can't take it any more.' I'm not too agile either, but then, I was never much of a sportsman. Second last in the marathon was probably my most memorable achievement.

Oddly enough, some of the most frequent visitors to my humble abode are honeymooners.

Why, I don't know, but they always ask for my blessing even though I am hardly an advertisement for married bliss. A seventy-year-old bachelor blessing a newly married couple? Maybe they are under the impression that I'm a Brahmachari? But how would that help them? They are going to have babies sooner or later.

It is seldom that they happen to be readers or book-lovers, so why pick an author, and that too one who does not go to places of worship? However, since these young couples are inevitably attractive, and full of high hopes for their future and the future of mankind, I am happy to talk to them, wish them well...and if it's a blessing they want, they are welcome. My hands are far from being saintly but at least they are well-intentioned.

I have, at times, been mistaken for other people.

'Are you Mr Pickwick?' asked a small boy. At least he'd been reading Dickens. A distant relative, I said, and beamed at him in my best Pickwickian manner.

I am at ease with children, who talk quite freely except

when accompanied by their parents. Then it's mum and dad who do all the talking.

'My son studies your book in school,' said one fond mother, proudly exhibiting her ten-year-old. 'He wants your autograph.'

'What's the name of the book you're reading?' I asked.

'Tom Sawyer,' he said promptly.

So I signed Mark Twain in his autograph book. He seemed quite happy.

A schoolgirl asked me to autograph her maths textbook.

'But I failed in maths,' I said. 'I'm just a story writer.'

'How much did you get?'

'Four out of a hundred.'

She looked at me rather crossly and snatched the book away.

I have signed books in the names of Enid Blyton, R.K. Narayan, Ian Botham, Daniel Defoe, Harry Potter and the Swiss Family Robinson. No one seems to mind.

Cricket for the Crocodile

R anji was up at dawn.

It was Sunday, a school holiday. Although he was supposed to be preparing for his exams, only a fortnight away, he couldn't resist one or two more games before getting down to history and algebra and other unexciting things.

'I'm going to be a Test cricketer when I grow up,' he told his mother. 'Of what use will maths be to me?'

'You never know,' said his mother, who happened to be more of a cricket fan than his father. 'You might need maths to work out your batting average. And as for history, wouldn't you like to be a part of history? Famous cricketers make history!'

'Making history is all right,' said Ranji. 'As long as I don't have to remember the date on which I make it!'

Ranji met his friends and teammates in the park. The grass was still wet with dew, the sun only just rising behind the distant hills. The park was full of flower-beds, and swings and slides for smaller children. The boys would have to play on the river bank against their rivals, the village boys. Ranji did not have a full team that morning, but he was looking for a 'friendly' match. The really important game would be held the following Sunday.

The village team was quite good because the boys lived near each other and practised a lot together, whereas Ranji's team was drawn from all parts of the town. There was the baker's boy, Nathu; the tailor's son, Sunder; the postmaster's son, Prem; and the bank manager's son, Anil. These were some of the better players. Sometimes their fathers also turned up for a game. The fathers weren't very good, but you couldn't tell them that. After all, they helped to provide bats and balls and pocket-money.

A regular spectator at these matches was Nakoo the crocodile, who lived in the river. Nakoo means Nosey, but the village boys were very respectful and called him Nakoo-ji, Nakoo, sir. He had a long snout, rows of ugly-looking teeth (some of them badly in need of fillings), and a powerful scaly tail.

He was nearly fifteen feet long, but you did not see much of him; he swam low in the water and glided smoothly through the tall grasses near the river. Sometimes he came out on the river bank to bask in the sun. He did not care for people, especially cricketers. He disliked the noise they made, frightening away the water-birds and other creatures required for an interesting menu, and it was also alarming to have cricket balls plopping around in the shallows where he liked to rest.

Once Nakoo crept quite close to the bank manager, who was resting against one of the trees near the river bank. The bank manager was a portly gentleman, and Nakoo seemed to think he would make a good meal. Just then a party of villagers had come along, beating drums for a marriage party. Nakoo retired to the muddy waters of the river. He was a little tired of swallowing frogs, eels and herons. That juicy bank manager would make a nice change—he'd grab him one day!

∽

The village boys were a little bigger than Ranji and his friends, but they did not bring their fathers along. The game made very little sense to the older villagers. And when balls came flying across fields to land in milk pails or cooking pots, they were as annoyed as the crocodile.

Today, the men were busy in the fields, and Nakoo the crocodile was wallowing in the mud behind a screen of reeds and water-lilies. How beautiful and innocent those lilies looked! Only sharp eyes would have noticed Nakoo's long snout thrusting above the broad flat leaves of the lilies. His eyes were slits. He was watching.

Ranji struck the ball hard and high. Splash! It fell into the river about thirty feet from where Nakoo lay. Village boys and town boys dashed into the shallow water to look for the ball. Too many of them! Crowds made Nakoo nervous. He slid away, crossed the river to the opposite bank, and sulked.

As it was a warm day, nobody seemed to want to get out of the water. Several boys threw off their clothes, deciding that it was a better day for swimming than for cricket. Nakoo's mouth watered as he watched those bare limbs splashing about.

'We're supposed to be practising,' said Ranji, who took his

cricket seriously. 'We won't win next week.'

'Oh, we'll win easily,' said Anil joining him on the river bank. 'My father says he's going to play.'

'The last time he played, we lost,' said Ranji. 'He made two runs and forgot to field.'

'He was out of form,' said Anil, ever loyal to his father, the bank manager.

Sheroo, the captain of the village team, joined them. 'My cousin from Delhi is going to play for us. He made a hundred in one of the matches there.'

'He won't make a hundred on this wicket,' said Ranji. 'It's slow at one end and fast at the other.'

'Can I bring my father?' asked Nathu, the baker's son.

'Can he play?'

'Not too well, but he'll bring along a basket of biscuits, buns and pakoras.'

'Then he can play,' said Ranji, always quick to make up his mind. No wonder he was the team's captain! 'If there are too many of us, we'll make him twelfth man.'

The ball could not be found, and as they did not want to risk their spare ball, the practice session was declared over.

'My grandfather's promised me a new ball,' said little Mani, from the village team, who bowled tricky leg-breaks which bounced off to the side.

'Does he want to play, too?' asked Ranji.

'No, of course not. He's nearly eighty.'

'That's settled then,' said Ranji. 'We'll all meet here at nine o'clock next Sunday. Fifty overs a side.'

They broke up, Sheroo and his team wandering back to

the village, while Ranji and his friends got onto their bicycles (two or three to a bicycle, since not everyone had one), and cycled back to town.

Nakoo, left in peace at last, returned to his favourite side of the river and crawled some way up the river bank, as if to inspect the wicket. It had been worn smooth by the players, and looked like a good place to relax. Nakoo moved across it. He felt pleasantly drowsy in the warm sun, so he closed his eyes for a little nap. It was good to be out of the water for a while.

∽

The following Sunday morning, a cycle bell tinkled at the gate. It was Nathu, waiting for Ranji to join him. Ranji hurried out of the house, carrying his bat and a thermos of lime juice thoughtfully provided by his mother.

'Have you got the stumps?' he asked.

'Sunder has them.'

'And the ball?'

'Yes. And Anil's father is bringing one too, provided he opens the batting!'

Nathu rode, while Ranji sat on the cross bar with bat and thermos. Anil was waiting for them outside his house.

'My father's gone ahead on his scooter. He's picking up Nathu's father. I'll follow with Prem and Sunder.'

Most of the boys got to the river bank before the bank manager and the baker. They left their bicycles under a shady banyan tree and ran down the gentle slope to the river. And then, one by one, they stopped, astonished by what they saw.

They gaped in awe at their cricket pitch.

Across it, basking in the soft warm sunshine, was Nakoo the crocodile.

'Where did it come from?' asked Ranji.

'Usually he stays in the river,' said Sheroo, who had joined them. 'But all this week he's been coming out to lie on our wicket. I don't think he wants us to play.'

'We'll have to get him off,' said Ranji.

'You'd better keep out of reach of his tail and jaws!'

'We'll wait until he goes away,' said Prem.

But Nakoo showed no signs of wanting to leave. He rather liked the smooth flat stretch of ground which he had discovered. And here were all the boys again, doing their best to disturb him.

After some time the boys began throwing pebbles at Nakoo. These had no effect, simply bouncing off the crocodile's tough hide. They tried mud balls and an orange. Nakoo twitched his tail and opened one eye, but refused to move on.

Then Prem took a ball, and bowled a fast one at the crocodile. It bounced just short of Nakoo and caught him on the snout. Startled and stung, he wriggled off the pitch and moved rapidly down the river bank and into the water. There was a mighty splash as he dived for cover.

'Well bowled, Prem!' said Ranji. 'That was a good ball.'

'Nakoo-ji will be in a bad mood after that,' warned Sheroo. 'Don't get too close to the river.'

The bank manager and the baker were the last to arrive. The scooter had given them some trouble. No one mentioned the crocodile, just in case the adults decided to call the match off.

After inspecting the wicket, which Nakoo had left in fair condition, Sheroo and Ranji tossed a coin. Ranji called 'Heads!'

but it came up tails. Sheroo chose to bat first.

The tall Delhi player came out to open the innings with little Mani.

Mani was a steady bat, who could stay at the wicket for a long time; but in a one-day match, quick scoring was needed. This the Delhi player provided. He struck a four, then took a single off the last ball of the over.

In the third over, Mani tried to hit out and was bowled for a duck. So the village team's score was 13 for 1.

'Well done,' said Ranji to fast bowler Prem. 'But we'll have to get that tall fellow out soon. He seems quite good.'

The tall fellow showed no sign of getting out. He hit two more boundaries and then swung one hard and high towards the river.

Nakoo, who had been sulking in the shallows, saw the ball coming towards him. He opened his jaws wide, and with a satisfying 'clunk!' the ball lodged between his back teeth.

Nakoo got his teeth deep into the cricket ball and chewed. Revenge was sweet. And the ball tasted good, too. The combination of leather and cork was just right. Nakoo decided that he would snap up any other balls that came his way.

'Harmless old reptile,' said the bank manager. He produced a new ball and insisted that he bowl with it.

It proved to be the most expensive over of the match. The bank manager's bowling was quite harmless and the Delhi player kept hitting the ball into the fields for fours and sixes. The score soon mounted to 40 for 1. The bank manager modestly took himself off.

By the time the tenth over had been bowled, the score had mounted to 70. Then Ranji, bowling slow spins, lost his grip on the ball and sent the batsman a full toss. Having played the good balls perfectly, the Delhi player couldn't resist taking a mighty swipe at the bad ball. He mistimed his shot and was astonished to see the ball fall into the hands of a fielder near the boundary. 70 for 2. The game was far from being lost for Ranji's team.

A couple of wickets fell cheaply, and then Sheroo came in and started playing rather well. His drives were straight and clean. The ball cut down the buttercups and hummed over the grass. A big hit landed in a poultry yard. Feathers flew and so did curses. Nakoo raised his head to see what all the noise was about. No further cricket balls came his way, and he gazed balefully at a heron who was staying just out of his reach.

The score mounted steadily. The fielding grew slack, as it often does when batsmen gain the upper hand. A catch was dropped. And Nathu's father, keeping wicket, missed a stumping chance.

'No more grown-ups in our team,' grumbled Nathu.

The baker made amends by taking a good catch behind the wicket. The score was 115 for 5, with about half the overs remaining.

Sheroo kept his end up, but the remaining batsmen struggled for runs and the end came with about 5 overs still to go. A modest total of 145.

'Should be easy,' said Ranji.

'No problem,' said Prem.

'Lunch first,' said the bank manager, and they took a half-hour break.

The village boys went to their homes for rest and refreshment, while Ranji and his team spread themselves out under the banyan tree.

Nathu's father had brought patties and pakoras; the bank manager brought a basket of oranges and bananas; Prem had brought a jack-fruit curry; Ranji had brought a halwa made from carrots, milk and sugar; Sunder had brought a large container full of savoury rice cooked with peas and fried onions; and the others had brought various curries, pickles and sauces. Everything was shared, and with the picnic in full swing no one noticed that Nakoo the crocodile had left the water. Using some tall reeds as cover, he had crept half-way up the river bank. Those delicious food smells had reached him too, and he was unwilling to be left out of the picnic. Perhaps the boys would leave something for him. If not...

'Time to start,' announced the bank manager, getting up. 'I'll open the batting. We need a good start if we are going to win!'

∽

The bank manager strode out to the wicket in the company of young Nathu. Sheroo opened the bowling for the village team.

The bank manager took a run off the first ball. He puffed himself up and waved his bat in the air as though the match had already been won. Nathu played out the rest of the over without taking any chances.

The tall Delhi player took up the bowling from the other end. The bank manager tapped his bat impatiently, then raised it above his shoulders, ready to hit out. The bowler took a long fast run up to the bowling crease. He gave a little leap, his arm swung over, and the ball came at the bank manager in a swift, curving flight.

The bank manager still had his bat raised when the ball flew past him and uprooted his middle stump.

A shout of joy went up from the fielders. The bank manager was on his way back to the shade of the banyan tree.

'A fly got in my eye,' he muttered. 'I wasn't ready. Flies everywhere!' And he swatted angrily at flies that no one else could see.

The villagers, hearing that someone as important as a bank manager was in their midst, decided that it would be wrong for him to sit on the ground like everyone else. So they brought him a cot from the village. It was one of those light wooden beds, taped with strands of thin rope. The bank manager lowered himself into it rather gingerly. It creaked but took his weight.

The score was 1 for 1.

Anil took his father's place at the wicket and scored ten runs in two overs. The bank manager pretended not to notice but he was really quite pleased. 'Takes after me,' he said, and made himself comfortable on the cot.

Nathu kept his end up while Anil scored the runs. Then Anil was out, skying a catch to mid wicket.

25 for 2 in six overs. It could have been worse.

'Well played!' called the bank manager to his son, and then lost interest in the proceedings. He was soon fast asleep on the cot. The flies did not seem to bother him any more.

Nathu kept going, and there were a couple of good

partnerships for the fourth and fifth wickets. When the Delhi player finished his share of overs, the batsmen became more free in their stroke-play. Then little Mani got a ball to spin sharply, and Nathu was caught by the wicket-keeper.

It was 75 for 4 when Ranji came in to bat.

Before he could score a run, his partner at the other end was bowled. And then Nathu's father strode up to the wicket, determined to do better than the bank manager. In this he succeeded by one run.

The baker scored two, and then in trying to run another two when there was only one to be had, found himself stranded half-way up the wicket. The wicket-keeper knocked his stumps down.

The boys were too polite to say anything. And as for the bank manager he was now fast asleep under the banyan tree.

So intent was everyone on watching the cricket that no one noticed that Nakoo the crocodile had crept further up the river bank to slide beneath the cot on which the bank manager was sleeping.

There was just room enough for Nakoo to get between the legs of the cot. He thought it was a good place to lie concealed, and he seemed not to notice the large man sleeping peacefully just above him.

Soon the bank manager was snoring gently, and it was not long before Nakoo dozed off, too. Only, instead of snoring, Nakoo appeared to be whistling through his crooked teeth.

75 for 5 and it looked as though Ranji's team would soon be

crashing to defeat.

Sunder joined Ranji and, to everyone's delight, played two lovely drives to the boundary. Then Ranji got into his stride and cut and drove the ball for successive fours. The score began to mount steadily. 112 for 5. Once again there were visions of victory.

After Sunder was out, stumped, Ranji was joined by Prem, a big hitter. Runs came quickly. The score reached 140. Only six runs were needed for victory.

Ranji decided to do it in style. Receiving a half-volley, he drove the ball hard and high towards the banyan tree.

Thump! It struck Nakoo on the jaw and loosened one of his teeth.

It was the second time that day he'd been caught napping. He'd had enough of it.

Nakoo lunged forward, tail thrashing and jaws snapping. The cot, with the manager still on it, rose with him. Crocodile and cot were now jammed together, and when Nakoo rushed forward, he took the cot with him.

The bank manager, dreaming that he was at sea in a rowing boat, woke up to find the cot pitching violently from side to side. 'Help!' he shouted. 'Help!'

The boys scattered in all directions, for the crocodile was now advancing down the wicket, knocking over stumps and digging up the pitch. He found an abandoned sun hat and swallowed it. A wicket-keeper's glove went the same way. A batsman's pad was caught up on his tail.

All this time the bank manager hung on to the cot for safety, but would he be able to get out of reach of Nakoo's jaw and tail? He decided to hang on to the cot until it was dislodged.

'Come on, boys, help!' he shouted. 'Get me off!'

But the cot remained firmly attached to the crocodile, and so did the bank manager.

The problem was solved when Nakoo made for the river and plunged into its familiar waters. Then the bank manager tumbled into the water and scrambled up the bank, while Nakoo made for the opposite shore.

The bank manager's ordeal was over, and so was the cricket match.

'Did you see how I dealt with that crocodile?' he said, still dripping, but in a better humour, now that he was safe again. 'By the way, who won the match?'

'We don't know,' said Ranji, as they trudged back to their bicycles. 'That would have been a six if you hadn't been in the way.'

Sheroo, who had accompanied them as far as the main road, offered a return match the following week.

'I'm busy next week,' said the baker.

'I have another game,' said the bank manager.

'What game is that, sir?' asked Ranji.

'Chess,' said the bank manager.

Ranji and his friends began making plans for the next match. 'You won't win without us,' said the bank manager. 'Not a chance,' said the baker.

But Ranji's team did, in fact, win the next match.

Nakoo the crocodile did not trouble them because the cot was still attached to his back, and it took him several weeks to get it off.

A number of people came to the river bank to look at the crocodile who carried his own bed around.

Some even stayed to watch the cricket.

Party Time in Mussoorie

It is very kind of people to invite me to their parties, especially as I do not throw parties myself, or invite anyone anywhere. At more than one party I have been known to throw things at people. Inspite of this—or maybe because of it—I get invited to these affairs.

I can imagine a prospective hostess saying 'Shall we invite Ruskin?'

'Would it be safe?' says her husband doubtfully. 'He has been known to throw plates at people.'

'Oh, then we must have him!' she shouts in glee. 'What fun it will be, watching him throw a plate at——. We'll use the cheaper crockery, of course...'

Here I am tempted to add that living in Mussoorie these forty odd years has been one long party. But if that were so, I would not be alive today. Rekha's garlic chicken and Nandu's shredded lamb would have done for me long ago. They have certainly done for my teeth. But they are only partly to blame.

Hill goats are tough, stringy creatures. I remember Begum Para trying to make us rogan josh one evening. She sat over the degchi for three or four hours but even then the mutton wouldn't become tender.

Begum Para, did I say?

Not the Begum Para? The saucy heroine of the silver screen? And why not? This remarkable lady had dropped in from Pakistan to play the part of my grandmother in Shubhadarshini's serial 'Ek Tha Rusty', based on stories of my childhood. Not only was she a wonderful actress, she was also a wonderful person who loved cooking. But she was defeated by the Mussoorie goat, who resisted all her endeavours to turn it into an edible rogan josh.

The Mussoorie goat is good only for getting into your garden and eating up your dahlias. These creatures also strip the hillside of any young vegetation that attempts to come up in the spring or summer. I have watched them decimate a flower garden and cause havoc to a vegetable plot. For this reason alone I do not shed a tear when I see them being marched off to the butcher's premises. I might cry over a slaughtered chicken, but not over a goat.

One of my neighbours on the hillside, Mrs K—, once kept a goat as a pet. She attempted to throw one or two parties, but no one would go to them. The goat was given the freedom of the drawing room and smelt to high heaven. Mrs K—was known to take it to bed with her. She too developed a strong odour. It is not surprising that her husband left the country and took a mistress in Panama. He couldn't get much further, poor man.

Mrs K—'s goat disappeared one day, and that same night

feast was held in Kolti village, behind Landour. People say the mutton was more tender and succulent than than at most feasts-the result, no doubt, of its having shared Mrs K—'s meals and bed for a couple of years.

One of Mrs K—'s neighbours was Mrs Santra, a kind-hearted but rather tiresome widow in her sixties. She was childless but had a fixation that, like the mother of John the Baptist, she would conceive in her sixties and give birth to a new messenger of the Messiah. Every month she would visit the local gynaecologist for advice, and the doctor would be gentle with her and tell her anything was possible and that in the meantime she should sustain herself with nourishing soups and savouries.

Mrs Santra liked giving little tea parties and I went to a couple of them. The sandwiches, samosas, cakes and jam tarts were delicious, and I expressed my appreciation. But then she took to visiting me at odd times, and I found this rather trying, as she would turn up while I was writing or sleeping or otherwise engaged. On one occasion, when I pretended I was not at home, she even followed me into the bathroom (where I had concealed myself) and scolded me for trying to avoid her.

She was a good lady, but I found it impossible to reciprocate her affectionate and even at times ardent overtures. So I had to ask her to desist from visiting me. The next day she sent her servant down with a small present—a little pot with a pansy growing in it!

On that happy note, I leave Mrs Santra and turn to other friends.

Such as Aunty Bhakti, a tremendous consumer of viands and victuals who, after a more than usually heavy meal at my former lodgings, retired to my Indian style lavatory to relieve herself. Ten minutes passed, then twenty, and still no sign of Aunty! My other luncheon guests, the Maharani Saheba of Jind, writer Bill Aitken and local pehelwan Maurice Alexander, grew increasingly concerned. Was Aunty having a heart attack or was she just badly constipated?

I went to the bathroom door and called out: 'Are you all right, Aunty?'

A silence, and then, in a quavering voice, 'I'm stuck!'

'Can you open the door?' I asked.

'It's open,' she said, 'but I can't move.'

I pushed open the door and peered in. Aunty, a heavily-built woman, had lost her balance and subsided backwards on the toilet, in the process jamming her bottom into the cavity!

'Give me a hand, Aunty,' I said, and taking her by the hand (the only time I'd ever been permitted to do so), tried my best to heave her out of her predicament. But she wouldn't budge.

I went back to the drawing room for help. 'Aunty's stuck,' I said, 'and I can't get her out.' The Maharani went to take a look. After all, they were cousins. She came back looking concerned. 'Bill,' she said, 'get up and help Ruskin extricate Aunty before she has a heart attack!'

Bill Aitken and I bear some resemblance to Laurel and Hardy. I'm Hardy, naturally. We did our best but Aunty Bhakti couldn't be extracted. So we called on the expertise of Maurice, our pehelwan, and forming a human chain or something of a tug of war team, we all pulled and tugged until Aunty Bhakti came out with a loud bang, wrecking my toilet in the process.

I must say she was not the sort to feel embarrassed.

Returning to the drawing-room, she proceeded to polish off half a brick of ice cream.

Another ice cream fiend is Nandu Jauhar who, at the time of writing, owns the Savoy in Mussoorie. At a marriage party, and in my presence he polished off thirty-two cups of ice cream and this after a hefty dinner.

The next morning he was as green as his favorite pistachio ice cream.

When admonished, all he could say was 'They were only small cups, you know.'

Nandu's eating exploits go back to his schooldays when (circa 1950) he held the Doon School record for consuming the largest number of mangoes—a large bucketful, all of five kilos—in one extended sitting.

'Could you do it again?' we asked him the other day.

'Only if they are Alfonsos,' he said 'And you have to pay for them.'

Fortunately for our pockets, and for Nandu's well-being, Alfonsos are not available in Mussoorie in December.

You must meet Rekha someday. She grows herbs now, and leads the quiet life, but in her heyday she gave some memorable parties, some of them laced with a bit of pot or marijuana. Rekha was a full-blooded American girl who had married into a well-known and highly respected Brahmin family and taken an Indian name. She was highly respected too, because she'd produced triplets at her first attempt at motherhood.

Some of her old Hippie friends often turned up at her house.

One of them, a French sitar player, wore a red sock on his left foot and a green sock on his right. His shoes were decorated with silver sequins. Another of her friends was an Australian film producer who had yet to produce a film. On one occasion I found the Frenchman and the Australian in Lakshmi's garden, standing in the middle of a deep hole they'd been digging.

I thought they were preparing someone's grave and asked them who it was meant for. They told me they were looking for a short cut to Australia, and carried on digging. As I never saw them again, I presume they came out in the middle of the great Australian desert. Yes, her pot was that potent!

I have never smoked pot, and have never felt any inclination to do so. One can get a great 'high' from so many other things— falling in love, or reading a beautiful poem, or taking in the perfume of a rose, or getting up at dawn to watch the morning sky and then the sunrise, or listening to great music, or just listening to bird song—it does seen rather pointless having to depend on artificial stimulants for relaxation; but human beings are a funny lot and will often go to great lengths to obtain the sort of things that some would consider rubbish.

I have no intention of adopting a patronizing, moralizing tone. I did, after all, partake of Rekha's bhang pakoras one evening before Diwali, and I discovered a great many stars that I hadn't seen before.

I was in such high spirits that I insisted on being carried home by the two most attractive girls at the party—Abha Saili and Shenaz Kapadia—and they, having also partaken of those magical pakoras, were only too happy to oblige.

They linked arms to form a sort of chariot-seat, and I sat

upon it (I was much lighter then) and was carried with great dignity and aplomb down Landour's upper Mall, stopping only now and then to remove the odd, disfiguring nameplate from an offending gate.

On our way down, we encountered a lady on her way up. Well, she looked like a lady to me, and I took off my cap and wished her good evening and asked where she was going at one o' clock in the middle of the night.

She sailed past us without deigning to reply.

'Snooty old bitch!' I called out. 'Just who is that midnight woman?' I asked Abha.

'It's not a woman,' said Abha. 'It's the circuit judge.'

'The circuit judge is taking a circuitous route home,' I commented. 'And why is he going about in drag?'

'Hush. He's not in drag. He's wearing his wig!'

'Ah well,' I said, 'Even judges must have their secret vices. We must live and let live!'

They got me home in style, and I'm glad I never had to come up before the judge. He'd have given me more than a wigging.

That was a few years ago. Our Diwalis are far more respectable now, and Rekha sends us sweets instead of pakoras. But those were the days, my friend. We thought they'd never end.

In fact, they haven't. It's still party-time in Landour and Mussoorie.

On the Road to Delhi

Road travel can involve delays and mishaps, but it also provides you with the freedom to stop where you like and do as you like. I have never found it boring. The seven-hour drive from Mussoorie to Delhi can become a little tiring towards the end, but as I do not drive myself, I can sit back and enjoy everything that the journey has to offer.

I have been to Delhi five times in the last six months—something of a record for me—and on every occasion I have travelled by road. I like looking at the countryside, the passing scene, the people along the road, and this is something I don't see any more from trains; those thick windows of frosted glass effectively cut me off from the world outside.

On my last trip we had to leave the main highway because of a disturbance near Meerut. Instead we had to drive through about a dozen villages in the prosperous sugarcane belt that dominates this area. It was a wonderful contrast, leaving the main road with its cafés, petrol pumps, factories and management institutes and entering the rural hinterland where very little had changed in a hundred years. Women worked in the fields, old men smoked hookahs in their courtyards, and a few children were playing guli-danda instead of cricket! It brought home to me the reality of India—urban life and rural life are still poles apart.

These journeys are seldom without incident. I was sipping a coffee at a wayside restaurant, when a foreign woman walked in, and asked the waiter if they had '*à la carte*'. Roadside stops seldom provide menus, nor do they go in for French, but our waiter wanted to be helpful, so he led the tourist outside and showed her the way to the public toilet. As she did not return to the restaurant, I have no idea if she eventually found *à la carte*.

My driver on a recent trip assured me that he knew Delhi very well and could get me to any destination. I told him I'd been booked into a big hotel near the airport, and gave him the name. Not to worry, he told me, and drove confidently towards Palam. There he got confused, and after taking several unfamiliar turnings, drove straight into a large piggery situated behind the airport. We were surrounded by some fifty or sixty pigs and an equal number of children from the mohalla. One boy even asked me if I wanted to purchase a pig. I do like bit of bacon now and then, but unlike Lord Emsworth I do not have any ambition to breed prize pigs, so I had to decline. After some arguments over right of way, we were allowed to proceed and finally made it to the hotel.

Occasionally I have shared a taxi with another passenger, but after one or two disconcerting experiences I have taken to travelling alone or with a friend.

The last time I shared a taxi with someone, I was pleased to find that my fellow passenger, a large gentleman with a fierce moustache, had bought one of my books, which was lying on the seat between us.

I thought I'd be friendly and so, to break the ice, I remarked 'I see you have one of my books with you,' glancing modestly at the paperback on the seat.

'What do you mean, your book?' he bridled, giving me a dirty look. 'I just bought this book at the news agency!'

'No, no,' I stammered, 'I don't mean it's mine, I mean it's my book—er, that is, I happened to write it!'

'Oh, so now you're claiming to be the author!' He looked at me as though I was a fraud of the worst kind. 'What is your real profession, may I ask?'

'I'm just a typist,' I said, and made no further attempt to make friends.

Indeed, I am very careful about trumpeting my literary or other achievements, as I am frequently misunderstood.

Recently, at a book reading in New Delhi, a little girl asked me how many books I'd written.

'Oh, about sixty or seventy,' I said quite truthfully.

At which another child piped up: 'Why can't you be a little modest about it?'

Sometimes you just can't win.

My author's ego received a salutary beating when on one of my earlier trips, I stopped at a small book-stall and looked around, hoping (like any other author) to spot one of my books. Finally, I found one, under a pile of books by Deepak Chopra, Khushwant Singh, William Dalrymple and other luminaries. I slipped it out from the bottom of the pile and surreptitiously placed it on top.

Unfortunately the bookseller had seen me do this.

He picked up the offending volume and returned it to the bottom of the pile, saying 'No demand for this book, sir'.

I wasn't going to tell him I was the author. But just to prove him wrong, I bought the poor neglected thing.

'This is a collector's item,' I told him.

'Ah,' he said, 'At last I meet a collector.'

∽

The number of interesting people I meet on the road is matched only by the number of interesting drivers who have carried me back and forth in their chariots of fire.

The last to do so, the driver of a Qualis, must have had ambitions to be an air pilot. He used the road as a runway and was constantly on the verge of taking off. Pedestrians, cyclists, and drivers of smaller vehicles scattered to left and right, often hurling abuse at my charioteer, who seemed immune to the most colourful invectives. Trucks did not give way but he simply swerved around them, adopting a zigzag approach to the task of getting from Delhi to Dehra Dun in the shortest possible time.

'There's no hurry,' I told him more than once, but his English was limited and he told me later that he thought I was saying 'Please hurry!'

Well, he hurried and he harried until at a railway-crossing where we were forced to stop, an irate scooterist came abreast and threatened to turn the driver over to the police. A long and heated argument followed, and it appeared that there would soon be a punch-up, when the crossing-gate suddenly opened and the Qualis flew forward, leaving the fuming scooterist far behind.

As I do not drive myself, I am normally the ideal person to have in the front seat; I repose complete confidence in the man behind the wheel. And sitting up front, I see more of the road and the passing scene.

One of Mussoorie's better drivers is Sardar Manmohan Singh who drives his own taxi. He is also a keen wildlife enthusiast. It always amazes me how he is able, to drive through the Siwaliks, on a winding hill road, and still be able to keep his eye open for denizens of the surrounding forest.

'See that cheetal!' he will exclaim, or 'What a fine sambhar!' or 'Just look at that elephant!'

All this at high speed. And before I've had time to get more than a fleeting glimpse of one of these creatures, we are well past them.

Manmohan swears that he has seen a tiger crossing the road near the Mohand Pass, and as he is a person of some integrity, I have to believe him. I think the tiger appears especially for Manmohan.

Another wildlife enthusiast is my old friend Vishal Ohri, of State Bank fame. On one occasion he drove me down a forest road between Haridwar and Mohand, and we did indeed see a number of animals, cheetal and wild boar.

Unlike our car drivers, he was in no hurry to reach our destination and would stop every now and then, in order to examine the footprints of elephants. He also pointed out large dollops of fresh elephant dung, proof that wild elephants were in the vicinity. I did not think his old Fiat would out-run an angry elephant and urged him to get a move on before nightfall.

Vishal then held forth on the benefits of elephant dung and how it could be used to reinforce mud walls. I assured him that I would try it out on the walls of my study, which was in danger of falling down.

Vishal was well ahead of his time. Only the other day I read in one of our papers that elephant dung could be converted into good quality paper. Perhaps they'll use it to make bank notes. Reserve Bank, please note.

∽

Other good drivers who have taken me here and there include Ganesh Saili, who is even better after a few drinks; Victor Banerjee who is better before drinks; and young Harpreet who is a fan of Kenny G's saxophone playing. On the road to Delhi with Harpreet, I had six hours of listening to Kenny G on tape. On my return, two days later, I had another six hours of Kenny G. Now I go into a frenzy whenever I hear a saxophone.

My publisher has an experienced old driver who also happens to be quite deaf. He blares the car horn vigorously and without respite. When I asked him why he used the horn so much, he replied, 'Well, I can't hear their horns, but I'll make sure they hear mine!' As good a reason as any.

It is sometimes said that women don't make good drivers, but I beg to differ. Mrs Biswas was an excellent driver but a dangerous woman to know. Her husband had been a well-known shikari, and he kept a stuffed panther in the drawing room of his Delhi farmhouse. Mrs Biswas spent the occasional weekend at her summer home in Landour. I'd been to one or two of her parties, attended mostly by menfolk.

One day, while I was loitering on the road, she drove up and asked me if I'd like to accompany her down to Dehra Dun.

'I'll come with you,' I said, 'provided we can have a nice lunch at Kwality.'

So down the hill we glided, and Mrs Biswas did some shopping, and we lunched at Kwality, and got back into her car and set off again—but in a direction opposite to Mussoorie and Landour.

'Where are we going?' I asked.

'To Delhi, of course. Aren't you coming with me?'

'I didn't know we were going to Delhi. I don't even have my pyjamas with me.'

'Don't worry,' said Mrs B. 'My husband's pyjamas will fit you.'

'He may not want me to wear his pyjamas,' I protested.

'Oh, don't worry. He's in London just now.'

I persuaded Mrs Biswas to stop at the nearest bus stop, bid her farewell, and took the bus back to Mussoorie. She may have been a good driver but I had no intention of ending up stuffed alongside the stuffed panther in the drawing room.

Mukesh Starts a Zoo

On a visit to Delhi with his parents, Mukesh spent two crowded hours at the zoo. He was dazzled by the many colourful birds, fascinated by the reptiles, charmed by the gibbons and chimps, and awestruck by the big cats—the lions, tigers and leopards. There was no zoo in the small town of Dehra where he lived, and the jungle was some way across the river-bed. So, as soon as he got home, he decided that he would have a zoo of his own.

'I'm going to start a zoo,' he announced at breakfast, the day after his return.

'But you don't have any birds or animals,' said Dolly, his little sister.

'I'll soon find them,' said Mukesh. 'That's what a zoo is all about—collecting animals.'

He was gazing at the white-washed walls of the verandah, where a gecko, a small wall lizard, was in pursuit of a fly. A little later Mukesh was trying to catch the lizard. But it was more alert than it looked, and always managed to keep a few inches ahead of his grasp.

'That's not the way to catch a lizard,' said Teju, appearing on the verandah steps. Teju and his sister Koki lived next door.

'You catch it, then,' said Mukesh.

Teju fetched a stick from the garden, where it had been used to prop up sweet-peas. He used the stick to tip the lizard off the wall and into a shoe-box.

'You'll be my Head Keeper,' said Mukesh, and soon he and Teju were at work in the back garden setting up enclosures with a roll of wire-netting they had found in the poultry shed.

'What else can we have in the zoo?' asked Teju. 'We need more than a lizard.'

'There's your grandmother's parrot,' said Mukesh.

'That's a good idea. But we won't tell her about it—not yet. I don't think she'd lend it to us. You see, it's a *religious* parrot. She's taught it lots of prayers and chants.'

'Then people are sure to come and listen to it. They'll pay, too.'

'We must have the parrot, then. What else?'

'Well, there's my dog,' said Mukesh. 'He's very fierce.'

'But a dog isn't a zoo animal.'

'Mine is—he's a wild dog. Look, he's black all over and he's got yellow eyes. There's no other dog like him.'

Mukesh's dog, who spent most of his time sleeping on the verandah, raised his head and obligingly revealed his yellow eyes.

'He's got jaundice,' said Teju. 'They've always been yellow.'

'All right, then, we've got a lizard, a parrot and a black dog with yellow eyes.'

'Koki has a white rabbit. Will she lend it to us?'

'I don't know. She thinks a lot of her rabbit. Maybe we can rent it from her.'

'And there's Sitaram's donkey.'

Sitaram, the dhobi-boy, usually used a donkey to deliver and collect the laundry from the houses along this particular street.

'Do you really want a donkey?' asked Teju doubtfully.

'Why not? It's a wild donkey. Haven't you heard of them?'

'I've heard of a wild ass, but not a wild donkey.'

'Well, they're all related to each other—asses, donkeys and mules.'

'Why don't you paint black stripes on it and call it a zebra?'

'No, that's cheating. It's got to be a proper zoo. No tricks—it's not a circus!'

On Saturday afternoon, a large placard with corrected spelling announced the opening of the zoo. It hung from the branches of the jack-fruit tree. Children were allowed in free but grown-ups had to buy tickets at fifty paise each, and Koki and Dolly were selling home-made tickets to the occasional passer-by or parent who happened to look in. Mukesh and his friends had worked hard at making notices for the various enclosures and each resident of the zoo was appropriately named.

The first attraction was a large packing-case filled with an assortment of house-lizards. They looked rather sluggish, having been generously fed with a supply of beetles and other insects.

Then came an enclosure in which Koki's white rabbit was on display. Freshly washed and brushed, it looked very cuddly and was praised by all.

Staring at it with evil intent from behind wire-netting was Mukesh's dog—RARE BLACK DOG WITH YELLOW EYES read the notice. Those yellow eyes were now trying hard to hypnotise the pink eyes of Koki's nervous rabbit. The dog pawed at the ground, trying to dig its way out from under the fence to get at the rabbit.

Tethered to a mango tree was Sitaram's small donkey. And tacked to the tree was a placard saying WILD ASS FROM KUTCH. A distant relative it may have been, but everyone recognised it as the local washerman's beast of burden. Every now and then it tried to break loose, for it was long past its feeding time.

There was also a duck that did not seem to belong to anyone, and a small cow that had strayed in on its own; but the star attraction was the parrot. As it could recite three different prayers, over and over again, it was soon surrounded by a group of admiring parents, all of whom wished they had a parrot who could pray, or rather, do their praying for them. Oddly enough, Koki's grandmother had chosen that day for visiting the temple, so she was unaware of the fuss that was being made of her pet, or even that it had been made an honorary member of the zoo. Teju had convinced himself she wouldn't mind.

While Mukesh and Teju were escorting visitors around the zoo, lecturing them on wild dogs and wild asses, Koki and Dolly were doing a brisk trade at the ticket counter. They had collected about ten rupees and were hoping for yet more, when there was a disturbance in the enclosures.

The black dog with yellow eyes had finally managed to dig his way out of his cage, and was now busy trying to dig his way into the rabbit's compartment. The rabbit was running round and round in panic-stricken circles. Meanwhile, the donkey had finally snapped the rope that held it and, braying loudly, scattered the spectators and made for home.

Koki went to the rescue of her rabbit and soon had it cradled in her arms. The dog now turned his attention to the duck. The duck flew over the packing-case, while the dog landed in it, scattering lizards in all directions.

In all this confusion, no one noticed that the door of the parrot's cage had slipped open. With a squawk and a whirr of wings, the bird shot out of the cage and flew off into a nearby orchard.

'The parrot's gone!' shouted Dolly, and almost immediately a silence fell upon the assembled visitors and children. Even the dog stopped barking. Granny's praying parrot had escaped! How could they possibly face her? Teju wondered if she would believe him if he told her it had flown off to heaven.

'Can anyone see it?' he asked tearfully.

'It's in a mango tree,' said Dolly. 'It won't come back.'

The crowd fell away, unwilling to share any of the blame when Koki's grandmother came home and discovered what had happened.

'What are we going to do now?' asked Teju, looking to Koki for help; but Koki was too upset to suggest anything. Mukesh had an idea.

'I know!' he said. 'We'll get another one!'

'How?'

'Well, there's the ten rupees we've collected. We can buy a new parrot for ten rupees!'

'But won't Granny know the difference?' asked Teju.

'All these hill parrots look alike,' said Mukesh.

So, taking the cage with them, they hurried off to the bazaar, where they soon found a bird-seller who was happy to sell them a parrot not unlike Granny's. He assured them it would talk.

'It looks like your grandmother's parrot,' said Mukesh on the way home. 'But can it pray?'

'Of course not,' said Koki. 'But we can teach it.'

Koki's grandmother, who was short-sighted, did not notice the substitution; but she complained bitterly that the bird had stopped repeating its prayers and was instead making rude noises and even swearing occasionally.

Teju soon remedied this sad state of affairs.

Every morning he stood in front of the parrot's cage and repeated Granny's prayers. Within a few weeks the bird had learnt to repeat one of them. Granny was happy again—not only because her parrot had started praying once more, but because Teju had started praying too!

The Boy Who Broke the Bank

Nathu, the sweeper-boy, grumbled to himself as he swept the steps of a small local bank, owned for the most part by Seth Govind Ram, a man of wealth whose haphazard business dealings had often brought him to the verge of ruin. Nathu used the small broom hurriedly and carelessly; the dust, after rising in a cloud above his head, settled down again on the steps. As Nathu was banging his pan against a dustbin, Sitaram, the washerman's son, passed by.

Sitaram was on his delivery round. He had a bundle of pressed clothes balanced on his head.

'Don't raise such a dust!' he called out to Nathu. 'Are you annoyed because they are still refusing to pay you another five rupees a month?'

'I don't want to talk about it,' complained the sweeper-boy. 'I haven't even received my regular pay. And this is the end of the month. Soon two months' pay will be due. Who would think this was a bank, holding up a poor man's salary?

As soon as I get my money, I'm off! Not another week will I work in the place.'

And Nathu banged his pan against the dustbin two or three times more, just to emphasise his point and give himself confidence.

'Well, I wish you luck,' said Sitaram. 'I'll be on the look-out for a new job for you.' And he plodded barefoot along the road, the big bundle of clothes hiding most of his head and shoulders.

At the fourth house he visited, delivering the washing, Sitaram overheard the woman of the house saying how difficult it was to get someone to sweep the courtyard. Tying up his bundle, Sitaram said: 'I know a sweeper-boy who's looking for work. He might be able to work for you from next month. He's with Seth Govind Ram's bank just now, but they are not giving him his pay, and he wants to leave.'

'Oh, is that so?' said Mrs Prakash. 'And why aren't they paying him?'

'They must be short of money,' said Sitaram with a shrug. Mrs Prakash laughed, 'Well, tell him to come and see me when he's free.'

Sitaram, glad that he had been of some service both to a friend and to a customer, hoisted his bag on his shoulders and went on his way.

Mrs Prakash had to do some shopping. She gave instructions to her maidservant with regard to the baby and told the cook what she wanted for lunch. Her husband worked for a large company, and they could keep servants and do things in style. Having given her orders, she set out for the bazaar to make her customary tour of the cloth shops.

A large, shady tamarind tree grew near the clock tower, and it was here that Mrs Prakash found her friend, Mrs Bhushan, sheltering from the heat. Mrs Bhushan was fanning herself with a large peacock's feather. She complained that the summer was the hottest in the history of the town. She then showed Mrs Prakash a sample of the cloth she was going to buy, and for five minutes they discussed its shade, texture and design.

When they had exhausted the subject, Mrs Prakash said:

'Do you know, my dear, Seth Govind Ram's bank can't even pay its employees. Only this morning I heard a complaint from their sweeper-boy, who hasn't received his pay for two months!'

'It's disgraceful!' exclaimed Mrs Bhushan. 'If they can't pay their sweeper, they must be in a bad way. None of the others can be getting paid either.'

She left Mrs Prakash at the tamarind tree and went in search of her husband, who was found sitting under the fan in Jugal Kishore's electrical goods shop, playing cards with the owner.

'So there you are!' cried Mrs Bhushan. 'I've been looking for you for nearly an hour. Where did you disappear to?'

'Nowhere,' replied Mr Bhushan. 'Had you remained stationary in one shop, you might have found me. But you go from one to another, like a bee in a flower-garden.'

'Now don't start grumbling. The heat is bad enough. I don't know what's happening to this town. Even the bank is going bankrupt.'

'What did you say?' said Mr Jugal Kishore, sitting up suddenly. 'Which bank?'

'Why, Seth Govind Ram's bank, of course. I hear they've stopped paying their employees—no salary for over three months! Don't tell me you have an account with them, Mr Kishore?'

'No, but my neighbour has!' he said, and he called out to the keeper of the barber shop next door: 'Faiz Hussain, have you heard the latest? Seth Govind Ram's bank is about to collapse! You'd better take your money out while there's still time.'

Faiz Hussain, who was cutting the hair of an elderly gentleman, was so startled that his hand shook and he nicked his customer's ear. The customer yelped with pain and distress: pain, because of the cut, and distress, because of the awful news he had just heard. With one side of his neck still unshorn, he leapt out of his chair and sped across the road to a general merchant's store, where there was a telephone. He dialled Seth Govind Ram's number. The Seth was not at home. Where was he, then? The Seth was holidaying in Kashmir. Oh, was that so? The elderly gentleman did not believe it. He hurried back to the barber shop and told Faiz Hussain: 'The bird has flown! Seth Govind Ram has left town. Definitely, it means a collapse. I'll have the rest of my haircut another time.' And he dashed out of the shop and made a bee-line for his office and cheque book.

∽

The news spread through the bazaar with the rapidity of a forest fire. From the general merchant's it travelled to the tea-shop, circulated amongst the customers, and then spread with them in various directions, to the paan-seller, the tailor, the fruit-vendor, the jeweller, the beggar sitting on the pavement .

Old Ganpat, the beggar, had a crooked leg and had been squatting on the pavement for years, calling for alms. In the evening someone would come with a barrow and take him away. He had never been known to walk. But now, on learning that the bank was about to collapse, Ganpat astonished everyone by leaping to his feet and actually running at a good speed in the direction of the bank. It soon became known that he had well over a thousand rupees in savings.

Men stood in groups at street corners, discussing the situation. There hadn't been so much excitement since India last won a Test Match. The small town in the foot-hills seldom had a crisis, never had floods or earthquakes or droughts. And so the imminent crash of the local bank set everyone talking and speculating and rushing about in a frenzy.

Some boasted of their farsightedness, congratulating themselves on having taken out their money, or on never putting any in. Others speculated on the reasons for the crash, putting it all down to Seth Govind Ram's pleasure-loving ways. The Seth had fled the state, said one. He had fled the country, said another. He had a South American passport, said a third. Others insisted that he was hiding somewhere in the town. And there was a rumour that he had hanged himself from the tamarind tree, where he had been found that morning by the sweeper-boy.

Someone who had a relative working as a clerk in the bank decided to phone him and get the facts.

'I don't know anything about it,' said the clerk, 'except that half the town is here, trying to take their money out. Everyone seems to have gone mad!'

'There's a rumour that none of you have been paid.'

'Well, all the clerks have had their salaries. We wouldn't be working otherwise. It may be that some of the part-time workers are getting paid late, but that isn't due to a shortage of money—only a few hundred rupees— it's just that the clerk who looks after their payments is on sick leave. You don't expect me to do his work, do you?' And he put the telephone down.

By afternoon the bank had gone through all its ready money, and the harassed manager was helpless. Emergency funds could only be obtained from one of the government banks, and now it was nearly closing time. He wasn't sure he could persuade the crowd outside to wait until the following morning. And Seth Govind Ram could be of no help from his luxury houseboat in Kashmir, five hundred miles away.

The clerks shut down their counters. But the people gathered outside on the steps of the bank, shouting: 'We want our money!' 'Give it to us today, break in!' 'Fetch Seth Govind Ram, we know he's hiding in the vaults!'

Mischief-makers, who did not have a paisa in the bank, joined the crowd. The manager stood at the door and tried to calm his angry customers. He declared that the bank had plenty of money, that they could withdraw all they wanted the following morning.

'We want it now!' chanted the people. 'Now, now, now!'

A few stones were thrown, and the manager retreated indoors, closing the iron-grilled gate.

A brick hurtled through the air and smashed into the plate-glass window which advertised the bank's assets.

Then the police arrived. They climbed the steps of the bank and, using their long sticks, pushed the crowd back until people began falling over each other. Gradually everyone dispersed, shouting that they would be back in the morning.

∽

Nathu arrived next morning to sweep the steps of the bank.

He saw the refuse and the broken glass and the stones cluttering up the steps. Raising his hands in horror, he cried: 'Goondas! Hooligans! May they suffer from a thousand ills! It was bad enough being paid irregularly—now I must suffer an increase of work!' He smote the steps with his broom, scattering the refuse.

'Good morning, Nathu,' said Sitaram, the washer-man's son, getting down from his bicycle. 'Are you ready to take up a new job from the first of next month? You'll have to, I suppose, now that the bank is closing.'

'What did you say?' said Nathu.

'Haven't you heard? The bank's gone bankrupt. You'd better hang around until the others arrive, and then start demanding your money too. You'll be lucky if you get it!' He waved cheerfully, and pedalled away on his bicycle.

Nathu went back to sweeping the steps, muttering to himself. When he had finished, he sat down on the bottom step to await the arrival of the manager. He was determined to get his pay.

'Who would have thought the bank would collapse,' he said to himself, and looked thoughtfully across the street. 'I wonder how it could have happened.'

The Trouble with Jinns

My friend Jimmy has only one arm. He lost the other when he was a young man of twenty-five. The story of how he lost his good right arm is a little difficult to believe, but I swear that it is absolutely true.

To begin with, Jimmy was (and presumably still is) a Jinn. Now a Jinn isn't really a human like us. A Jinn is a spirit creature from another world who has assumed, for a lifetime, the physical aspect of a human being. Jimmy was a true Jinn and he had the Jinn's gift of being able to elongate his arm at will. Most Jinns can stretch their arms to a distance of twenty or thirty feet. Jimmy could attain forty feet. His arm would move through space or up walls or along the ground like a beautiful gliding serpent. I have seen him stretched out beneath a mango tree, helping himself to ripe mangoes from the top of the tree. He loved mangoes. He was a natural glutton and it was probably his gluttony that first led him to misuse his peculiar gifts.

We were at school together at a hill station in northern

India. Jimmy was particularly good at basketball. He was clever enough not to lengthen his arm too much because he did not want anyone to know that he was a Jinn. In the boxing ring he generally won his fights. His opponents never seemed to get past his amazing reach. He just kept tapping them on the nose until they retired from the ring bloody and bewildered.

It was during the half-term examinations that I stumbled on Jimmy's secret. We had been set a particularly difficult algebra paper but I had managed to cover a couple of sheets with correct answers and was about to forge ahead on another sheet when I noticed someone's hand on my desk. At first I thought it was the invigilator's. But when I looked up there was no one beside me.

Could it be the boy sitting directly behind? No, he was engrossed in his question paper and had his hands to himself. Meanwhile, the hand on my desk had grasped my answer sheets and was cautiously moving off. Following its descent, I found that it was attached to an arm of amazing length and pliability. This moved stealthily down the desk and slithered across the floor, shrinking all the while, until it was restored to its normal length. Its owner was of course one who had never been any good at algebra.

I had to write out my answers a second time but after the exam I went straight up to Jimmy, told him I didn't like his game and threatened to expose him. He begged me not to let anyone know, assured me that he couldn't really help himself, and offered to be of service to me whenever I wished. It was tempting to have Jimmy as my friend, for with his long reach he would obviously be useful. I agreed to overlook the matter of the pilfered papers and we became the best of pals.

It did not take me long to discover that Jimmy's gift was more of a nuisance than a constructive aid. That was because Jimmy had a second-rate mind and did not know how to make proper use of his powers. He seldom rose above the trivial. He used his long arm in the tuck shop, in the classroom, in the dormitory. And when we were allowed out to the cinema, he used it in the dark of the hall.

Now the trouble with all Jinns is that they have a weakness for women with long black hair. The longer and blacker the hair, the better for Jinns. And should a Jinn manage to take possession of the woman he desires, she goes into a decline and her beauty decays. Everything about her is destroyed except for the beautiful long black hair.

Jimmy was still too young to be able to take possession in this way, but he couldn't resist touching and stroking long black hair. The cinema was the best place for the indulgence of his whims. His arm would start stretching, his fingers would feel their way along the rows of seats, and his lengthening limb would slowly work its way along the aisle until it reached the back of the seat in which sat the object of his admiration. His hand would stroke the long black hair with great tenderness and if the girl felt anything and looked round, Jimmy's hand would disappear behind the seat and lie there poised like the hood of a snake, ready to strike again.

At college two or three years later, Jimmy's first real victim succumbed to his attentions. She was a lecturer in economics, not very good looking, but her hair, black and lustrous, reached almost to her knees. She usually kept it in plaits but Jimmy saw her one morning just after she had taken a head bath, and her hair lay spread out on the cot on which she was reclining. Jimmy could no longer control himself. His spirit, the very essence of his personality, entered the woman's body and the next day she was distraught, feverish and excited. She would not eat, went into a coma, and in a few days dwindled to a mere skeleton. When she died, she was nothing but skin and bone but her hair had lost none of its loveliness.

I took pains to avoid Jimmy after this tragic event. I could not prove that he was the cause of the lady's sad demise but in my own heart I was quite certain of it. For since meeting Jimmy, I had read a good deal about Jinns and knew their ways.

We did not see each other for a few years. And then, holidaying in the hills last year, I found we were staying at the same hotel. I could not very well ignore him and after we had drunk a few beers together I began to feel that I had perhaps misjudged Jimmy and that he was not the irresponsible Jinn I had taken him for. Perhaps the college lecturer had died of some mysterious malady that attacks only college lecturers and Jimmy had nothing at all to do with it.

We had decided to take our lunch and a few bottles of beer to a grassy knoll just below the main motor road. It was late afternoon and I had been sleeping off the effects of the beer when I woke to find Jimmy looking rather agitated.

'What's wrong?' I asked.

'Up there, under the pine trees,' he said. 'Just above the road. Don't you see them?'

'I see two girls,' I said. 'So what?'

'The one on the left. Haven't you noticed her hair?'

'Yes, it is very long and beautiful and—now look, Jimmy, you'd better get a grip on yourself!' But already his hand was out of sight, his arm snaking up the hillside and across the road.

Presently I saw the hand emerge from some bushes near the girls and then cautiously make its way to the girl with the black tresses. So absorbed was Jimmy in the pursuit of his favourite pastime that he failed to hear the blowing of a horn. Around the bend of the road came a speeding Mercedes Benz truck.

Jimmy saw the truck but there wasn't time for him to shrink his arm back to normal. It lay right across the entire width of the road and when the truck had passed over it, it writhed and twisted like a mortally wounded python.

By the time the truck driver and I could fetch a doctor, the arm (or what was left of it) had shrunk to its ordinary size. We took Jimmy to hospital where the doctors found it necessary to amputate. The truck driver, who kept insisting that the arm he ran over was at least thirty feet long, was arrested on a charge of drunken driving.

Some weeks later I asked Jimmy, 'Why are you so depressed? You still have one arm. Isn't it gifted in the same way?'

'I never tried to find out,' he said, 'and I'm not going to try now.'

He is, of course, still a Jinn at heart and whenever he sees a girl with long black hair he must be terribly tempted to try out his one good arm and stroke her beautiful tresses. But he has learnt his lesson. It is better to be a human without any gifts than a Jinn or a genius with one too many.

Breakfast Time

I like a good sausage, I do;
It's a dish for the chosen and few.
Oh, for sausage and mash,
And of mustard a dash,
And an egg nicely fried—maybe two?
At breakfast or lunch, or at dinner,
The sausage is always a winner;
If you want a good spread,
Go for sausage on bread,
And forget all your vows to be slimmer.

'In Praise of the Sausage'
(Written for Victor and Maya Banerjee,
who excel at making sausage breakfasts.)

There is something to be said for breakfast.
If you take an early morning walk down Landour Bazaar,
you might be fortunate enough to see a very large cow standing

in the foyer of a hotel, munching on a succulent cabbage or cauliflower. The owner of the hotel has a soft spot for this particular cow, and invites it in for breakfast every morning. Having had its fill, the cow—very well-behaved—backs out of the shop and makes way for paying customers.

I am not one of them. I prefer to have my breakfast at home—a fried egg, two or three buttered toasts, a bit of bacon if I'm lucky, otherwise some fish pickle from the south, followed by a cup of strong coffee—and I'm a happy man and can take the rest of the day in my stride.

I don't think I have ever written a good story without a good breakfast. There are, of course, writers who do not eat before noon. Both they and their prose have a lean and hungry look. Dickens was good at describing breakfasts and dinners— especially Christmas repasts—and many of his most rounded characters were good-natured people who were fond of their food and drink—Mr Pickwick, the Cheeryble brothers, Mr Weller senior, Captain Cuttle—as opposed to the half-starved characters in the works of some other Victorian writers. And remember, Dickens had an impoverished childhood. So I took it as a compliment when a little girl came up to me the other day and said, 'Sir, you're Mr Pickwick!'

As a young man, I had a lean and hungry look. After all, I was often hungry. Now if I look like Pickwick, I take it as an achievement.

And all those breakfasts had something to do with it.

It's not only cows and early-to-rise writers who enjoy a good breakfast. Last summer, Colonel Solomon was out taking his pet Labrador for an early morning walk near Lal Tibba when a leopard sprang out of a thicket, seized the dog and made off with it down the hillside. The dog did not even have time to yelp. Nor did the Colonel. Suffering from shock, he left Landour the next day and has yet to return.

Another leopard—this time at the other end of Mussoorie—entered the Savoy hotel at dawn, and finding nothing in the kitchen except chicken's feathers, moved on to the billiard room and there vented its frustration on the cloth of the billiard table, clawing it to shreds. The leopard was seen in various parts of the hotel before it made off in the direction of the Ladies' Block.

Just a hungry leopard in search of a meal. But three days later, Nandu Jauhar, the owner of the Savoy, found himself short of a lady housekeeper. Had she eloped with the laundryman, or had she become a good breakfast for the leopard? We do not know till this day.

English breakfasts, unlike continental breakfasts, are best enjoyed in India where you don't have to rush off to catch a bus or a train or get to your office in time. You can linger over your scrambled egg and marmalade on toast. What would breakfast be without some honey or marmalade? You can have an excellent English breakfast at the India International Centre, where I have spent many pleasant reflective mornings... And a super breakfast at the Raj Mahal Hotel in Jaipur. But some hotels give very inferior breakfasts, and I am afraid that certain Mussoorie establishments are great offenders, specializing in singed omelettes and burnt toasts.

Many people are under the erroneous impression that the days of the British Raj were synonymous with huge meals and unlimited food and drink. This may have been the case in the days of the East India Company, but was far from being so during the last decade of British rule. Those final years coincided with World War II, when food rationing was in force. At my boarding school in Shimla, omelettes were made from powdered eggs, and the contents of the occasional sausage were very mysterious—so much so, that we called our sausages 'sweet mysteries of life!' after a popular Nelson Eddy song.

Things were not much better at home. Just porridge (no eggs!) bread and jam (no butter!), and tea with *ghur* instead of refined sugar. The *ghur* was, of course, much healthier than sugar.

Breakfasts are better now, at least for those who can afford them. The jam is better than it used to be. So is the bread. And I can enjoy a fried egg, or even two, without feeling guilty about it. But good omelettes are still hard to come by. They shouldn't be made in a hurried or slapdash manner. Some thought has to go into an omelette. And a little love too. It's like writing a book—done much better with some feeling!

Be Prepared

I was a Boy Scout once, although I couldn't tell a slip knot from a granny knot, nor a reef knot from a thief knot. I did know that a thief knot was to be used to tie up a thief, should you happen to catch one. I have never caught a thief—and wouldn't know what to do with one since I can't tie the right knot. I'd just let him go with a warning, I suppose. And tell him to become a Boy Scout.

'Be prepared!' That's the Boy Scout motto. And it is a good one, too. But I never seem to be well prepared for anything, be it an exam or a journey or the roof blowing off my room. I get halfway through a speech and then forget what I have to say next. Or I make a new suit to attend a friend's wedding, and then turn up in my pyjamas.

So, how did I, the most impractical of boys, survive as a Boy Scout?

Well, it seems a rumour had gone around the junior school (I was still a junior then) that I was a good cook. I had never cooked anything in my life, but of course I had spent a lot of time in the tuck shop making suggestions and advising Chimpu, who ran the tuck shop, and encouraging him to make more and better samosas, jalebies, tikkees and pakoras. For my unwanted advice, he would favour me with an occasional free samosa. So, naturally, I looked upon him as a friend and benefactor. With this qualification, I was given a cookery badge and put in charge of our troop's supply of rations.

There were about twenty of us in our troop. During the summer break our Scoutmaster, Mr Oliver, took us on a camping expedition to Taradevi, a temple-crowned mountain a few miles outside Shimla. That first night we were put to work, peeling potatoes, skinning onions, shelling peas and pounding masalas. These various ingredients being ready, I was asked, as the troop cookery expert, what should be done with them.

'Put everything in that big degchi,' I ordered. 'Pour half a tin of ghee over the lot. Add some nettle leaves, and cook for half an hour.'

When this was done, everyone had a taste, but the general opinion was that the dish lacked something. 'More salt,' I suggested.

More salt was added. It still lacked something. 'Add a cup of sugar,' I ordered.

Sugar was added to the concoction, but it still lacked something.

'We forgot to add tomatoes,' said one of the Scouts. 'Never mind,' I said. 'We have tomato sauce. Add a bottle of tomato sauce!'

'How about some vinegar?' suggested another boy. 'Just the

thing,' I said. 'Add a cup of vinegar!'

'Now it's too sour,' said one of the tasters.

'What jam did we bring?' I asked.

'Gooseberry jam.'

'Just the thing. Empty the bottle!'

The dish was a great success. Everyone enjoyed it, including Mr Oliver, who had no idea what had gone into it.

'What's this called?' he asked.

'It's an all-Indian sweet-and-sour jam-potato curry,' I ventured.

'For short, just call it Bond bhujjia,' said one of the boys. I had earned my cookery badge!

Poor Mr Oliver; he wasn't really cut out to be a Scoutmaster, any more than I was meant to be a Scout.

The following day, he told us he would give us a lesson in tracking. Taking a half-hour start, he walked into the forest, leaving behind him a trail of broken twigs, chicken feathers, pine cones and chestnuts. We were to follow the trail until we found him.

Unfortunately, we were not very good trackers. We did follow Mr Oliver's trail some way into the forest, but then we were distracted by a pool of clear water. It looked very inviting. Abandoning our uniforms, we jumped into the pool and had a great time romping about or just lying on its grassy banks and enjoying the sunshine. Many hours later, feeling hungry, we returned to our campsite and set about preparing the evening meal. It was Bond bhujjia again, but with a few variations.

It was growing dark, and we were beginning to worry about Mr Oliver's whereabouts when he limped into the camp, assisted by a couple of local villagers. Having waited for us at the far end of the forest for a couple of hours, he had decided to return by following his own trail, but in the gathering gloom he was soon lost. Village folk returning home from the temple took charge and escorted him back to the camp. He was very angry and made us return all our good-conduct and other badges, which he stuffed into his haversack. I had to give up my cookery badge.

An hour later, when we were all preparing to get into our sleeping bags for the night, Mr Oliver called out, 'Where's dinner?'

'We've had ours,' said one of the boys. 'Everything is finished, sir.'

'Where's Bond? He's supposed to be the cook. Bond, get up and make me an omelette.'

'I can't, sir.'

'Why not?'

'You have my badge. Not allowed to cook without it. Scout rule, sir.'

'I've never heard of such a rule. But you can take your badges, all of you. We return to school tomorrow.'

Mr Oliver returned to his tent in a huff.

But I relented and made him a grand omelette, garnishing it with dandelion leaves and a chilli.

'Never had such an omelette before,' confessed Mr Oliver.

'Would you like another, sir?'

'Tomorrow, Bond, tomorrow. We'll breakfast early tomorrow.'

But we had to break up our camp before we could do that because in the early hours of the next morning, a bear strayed into our camp, entered the tent where our stores were kept, and created havoc with all our provisions, even rolling our biggest degchi down the hillside.

In the confusion and uproar that followed, the bear entered Mr Oliver's tent (our Scoutmaster was already outside, fortunately) and came out entangled in his dressing gown. It then made off towards the forest, a comical sight in its borrowed clothes.

And though we were a troop of brave little scouts, we thought it better to let the bear keep the gown.

Simply Living

These thoughts and observations were noted in my diaries through the 1980s, and may give readers some idea of the ups and downs, highs and lows, during a period when I was still trying to get established as an author.

March 1981

After a gap of twenty years, during which it was, to all practical purposes forgotten, *The Room on the Roof* (my first novel) gets reprinted in an edition for schools.

(This was significant, because it marked the beginning of my entry into the educational field. Gradually, over the years, more of my work became familiar to school children throughout the country.)

Stormy weather over Holi. Room flooded. Everyone taking turns with septic throats and fever. While in bed, read Stendhal's *Scarlet and Black*. I seem to do my serious reading only when I'm sick.

Felt well enough to take a leisurely walk down the Tehri

Road. Trees in new leaf. The fresh light green of the maples is very soothing.

I may not have contributed anything towards the progress of civilisation, but neither have I robbed the world of anything. Not one tree or bush or bird. Even the spider on my wall is welcome to his (her) space. Provided he (she) stays on the wall and does not descend on my pillow.

April

Swifts are busy nesting in the roof and performing acrobatics outside my window. They do everything on the wing, it seems— including feeding and making love. Mating in midair must be quite a feat.

Someone complimented me because I was 'always smiling'. I thought better of him for the observation and invited him over. Flattery will get you anywhere!

(This is followed by a three-month gap in my diary, explained by my next entry.)

Shortage of cash. Muddle, muddle, toil and trouble. I don't see myself—smiling.

Learn to zigzag. Try something different.

August

Kept up an article a day for over a month. Grub Street again!

DARE

WILL

KEEP SILENCE

These words helped Napoleon, but will they help me?

Try Cursing!

I curse the block to money.

I curse the thing that takes all my effort away.

I curse all that would make me a slave.

I curse those who would harm my loved ones.

And now stop cursing and give thanks for all the good things you have enjoyed in life.

'We should not spoil what we have by desiring what we have not, but remember that what we have was the gift of fortune.' (Epicurus)

〜

'We ought to have more sense, of course, than to try to touch a dream, or to reach that place which exists but in the glamour of a name.'

(H.M.Tomlinson, *Tide Marks*)

October

A good year for the cosmos flower. Banks of them everywhere. They like the day-long sun. Clean and fresh—my favourite flower *en-masse*.

But by itself, the wild commelina, sky-blue against dark green, always catches at the heart.

A latent childhood remains tucked away in our subconscious. This I have tried to explore...

A...stretches out on the bench like a cat, and the setting sun is trapped in his eyes, golden brown, glowing like tiger's eyes. (Oddly enough, this beautiful youth grew up to become a very sombre-looking padre.)

December

A kiss in the dark—warm and soft and all-encompassing—the moment stayed with me for a long time.

Wrote a poem, 'Who kissed me in the dark?' but it could not do justice to the kiss. Tore it up!

On the night of the 7th, light snowfall. The earliest that I can remember it snowing in Landour. Early morning, the hillside looked very pretty, with a light mantle of snow covering trees, rusty roofs, vehicles at the bus stop—and concealing our garbage dump for a couple of hours, until it melted.

January 1982

Three days of wind, rain, sleet and snow. Flooded out of my bedroom. We convert dining room into dormitory. Everything is bearable except the wind, which cuts through these old houses like a knife—under the roof, through flimsy verandah enclosures and ill-fitting windows, bringing the icy rain with it.

Fed up with being stuck indoors. Walked up to Lal Tibba, in flurries of snow. Came back and wrote the story 'The Wind on Haunted Hill'.

I invoke Lakshmi, who shines like the full moon.

Her fame is all-pervading.

Her benevolent hands are like lotuses.

I take refuge in her lotus feet.

Let her destroy my poverty forever.

Goddess, I take shelter at your lotus feet.

February

My boyhood was difficult, but I had my dreams to sustain me. What does one dream about now?

But sometimes, when all else fails, a sense of humour comes to the rescue.

And the children (Raki, Muki, Dolly) bring me joy. All children do. Sometimes I think small children are the only sacred things left on this earth. Children and flowers.

Further blasts of wind and snow. In spite of the gloom, wrote a new essay.

March

Blizzard in the night. Over a foot of snow in the morning. And so it goes on...unprecedented for March. The Jupiter effect? At least the snow prevents the roof from blowing away, as happened last year. Facing east (from where the wind blows) doesn't help. And it's such a rickety old house.

ↄ

Mid-March and the first warm breath of approaching summer. Risk a haircut. Ramkumar does his best to make me look like a 1930s film star. I suppose I ought to try another barber, but he's too nice. 'I look rather strange,' I said afterwards (like Wallace Beery in *Billy the Kid*). 'Don't worry,' he said. 'You'll get used to it.'

'Why don't you give me an Amitabh Bachchan haircut?'

'You'll need more hair for that,' he says.

ↄ

Bus goes down the mud, killing several passengers. Death moves about at random, without discriminating between the innocent and the evil, the poor and the rich. The only difference is that the poor usually handle it better.

Late March

The blackest cloud I've ever seen squatted over Mussoorie, and then it hailed marbles for half-an-hour. Nothing like a hailstorm to clear the sky. Even as I write, I see a rainbow forming.

And Goddess Lakshmi smiles on me. An unprecedented flow of cheques, mainly accrued royalties on 'Angry River' and 'The Blue Umbrella'. A welcome change from last year's shortages and difficulties.

Perfection

The smallest insect in the world is a sort of fairy-fly and its body is only a fifth of a millimetre long. One can only just see it with the naked eye. Almost like a speck of dust, yet it has perfect little wings and little combs on its legs for preening itself.

Late April

Abominable cloud and chilly rain. But Usha brings bunches of wild roses and irises. And her own gentle smile.

Mid-May

Raki (after reading my bio-data): 'Dada, you were born in 1934! And you are still here!' After a pause: 'You are very lucky.'

I guess I am, at that.

June

Did my sixth essay for *The Monitor* this year.

(Have written off and on, for *The Christian Science Monitor* of Boston from 1965 to 2002).

Wrote an article for a new magazine, *Keynote*, published in Bombay, and edited by Leela Naidu, Dom Moraes and David Davidar. It was to appear in the August issue. Now I'm told that the magazine has folded. (But David Davidar went on to bigger things with Penguin India!)

If at first you don't succeed, so much for sky-diving.

July

Monsoon downpour. Bedroom wall crumbling. Landslide cuts off my walk down the Tehri road.

Usha: a complexion like apricot blossom seen through a mist.

September

Two dreams:

A constantly recurring dream or rather, nightmare—I am forced to stay longer than I had intended in a very expensive hotel and know that my funds are insufficient to meet the bill. Fortunately, I have always woken up before the bill is presented!

Possible interpretation: fear of insecurity. My own variation of the dream, common to many, of falling from a height but waking up before hitting the ground.

Another occasional dream: living in a house perched over

a crumbling hillside. This one is not far removed from reality!

∽

Glorious day. Walked up and around the hill, and got some of the cobwebs out of my head.

That man is strongest who stands alone!

Some epigrams (for future use).

A well-balanced person: someone with a chip on both shoulders.

Experience: the knowledge that enables you to recognize a mistake when you make it the second time.

Sympathy: what one woman offers another in exchange for details.

Worry: the interest paid on trouble before it becomes due.

October

Some disappointment, as usual in connection with films (the screenplay I wrote for someone who wanted to remake *Kim*), but if I were to let disappointments get me down, I'd have given up writing twenty-five years ago.

A walk in the twilight. Soothing. Watched the winter-line from the top of the hill.

Raki first in school races.

Savitri (Dolly) completes two years. Bless her fat little toes.

Advice to myself: conserve energy. Talk less!

'Better to have people wondering why you don't speak than to have them wondering why you speak.' (Disraeli)

∽

Wrote 'The Funeral'. One of my better stories, and thus more difficult to place.

If death was a thing that money could buy,
The rich they would live, and the poor they would die.

In California, you can have your body frozen after death in the hope that a hundred years from now some scientist will come along and bring you to life again. You pay in advance, of course.

December

I never have much luck with films or film-makers. Mr K.S. Varma finally (after five years) completed his film of my story 'The Last Tiger', but could not find a distributor for it. I don't regret the small sum I received for the story. He ran out of money—and tigers!—and apparently went to heroic lengths to complete the film in the forests of Bihar and Orissa. He used a circus tiger for the more intimate scenes, but this tiger disappeared one day, along with one of the actors. Tom Alter played a shikari and went on to play other, equally hazardous roles: he's still around, the tiger having spared him, but the film was never seen (and hasn't been seen to this day).

A last postcard from an old friend: 'Ruskin, dear friend—but you won't be, unless you keep your word about lunching with us on Xmas Day. PLEASE DO COME, both Kanshi and I need your presence. It will be a small party this time as most of our friends are either *hors-de-combat* or dead! Bring Rakesh and

Mukesh. Please let me know. I have been in bed for two days with a chill. Please don't disappoint.

Love,

Winnie'

(We did go to the Christmas party, but sadly, the chill became pneumonia and there were no more parties with Winnie and Kanshi, who were such good company. I still miss them.)

January 1984

To Maniram's home near Lal Tibba. He was brought up by his grandmother—his mother died when he was one. Keeps two calves, two cows (one brindled), and a pup of indeterminate breed. Made me swallow a glass of milk. Haven't touched milk for years, can't stand the stuff, but drank it so as not to hurt his feelings. (Mani and his Granny turned up in my children's story *Getting Granny's Glasses*.)

∽

On the 6th it was bitterly cold, and the snow came in through my bedroom roof. Not enough money to go away, but at least there's enough for wood and coal. I hate the cold—but the children seem to enjoy it. Raki, Muki and Dolly in constant high spirits.

∽

February

Two days and nights of blizzard—howling winds, hail, sleet, snow. Prem bravely goes out for coal and kerosene oil. Worst weather we've ever had up here. Sick of it.

~

March

Peach, plum and apricot trees in blossom. Gentle weather at last. Schools reopen.

Sold German and Dutch translation rights in a couple of my children's books. I wish I could write something of lasting worth. I've done a few good stories but they are so easily lost in the mass of wordage that pours forth from the world's presses.

Here are some statistics which I got from the U.K. a couple of years ago:

There are over nine million books in the British Museum and they fill 86 miles of shelving.

There are over 50,000 living British authors. They don't get rich. The latest Society of Authors survey shows that only 55 per cent of those whose main occupation is writing earn over £700 a year.

Britain has 8,500 booksellers, as well as many other shops where books are sold.

The first book to be printed in Britain was *The Dictes and Sayings of the Philosophers*, which was translated and printed by William Caxton in 1477.

As many books were published in Britain between 1940 and 1980 as in the five centuries from Caxton's first book.

Who says the reading habit is dying?

~

April

The 'adventure wind' of my boyhood—I felt it again today. Walked five miles to Suakholi, to look at an infinity of mountains.

The feeling of space—limitless space—can only be experienced by living in the mountains.

It is the emotional, the spiritual surge, that draws us back to the mountains again and again. It was not altogether a matter of mysticism or religion that prompted the ancients to believe that their gods dwelt in the high places of this earth. Those gods, by whatever name we know them, still dwell there. From time to time we would like to be near them, that we may know them and ourselves more intimately.

May

Completed my half century and launched into my 51st year.

Fifty is a dangerous age for most men. Last year there was nothing to celebrate, and at the end of it my diary went into the dustbin. There was an abortive and unhappy love affair (dear reader, don't fall in love at fifty!), a crisis in the home (with Prem missing for weeks), conflicts with publishers, friends, myself. So skip being fifty. Become fifty-one as soon its possible; you will find yourself in calmer waters. If you fall in love at the age of fifty, inner turmoil and disappointment is almost guaranteed. Don't listen to what the wise men say about love. P.G. Wodehose said the whole thing more succinctly: 'You know, the way love can change a fellow is really frightful to contemplate.' Especially when a fifty-year-old starts behaving like a sixteen-year-old!

Most of my month's earnings went to the dentist. And I notice he's wearing a new suit.

June

A name—a lovely face—turn back the years: 45 years to be exact, when I was a small boy in Jamnagar, where my father taught English to some of the younger princes and princesses—among them M—whose picture I still have in my album (taken by my father). She wrote to me after reading something I'd written, wanting to know if I was the same little boy, i.e., Mr Bond's mischievous son. I responded, of course. A link with my father is so rare; and besides, I had a crush on her. My first love! So long ago—but it seems like yesterday...

ഗ

Monsoon breaks.

Money-drought breaks.

And if there's a connection, may the rain gods be generous this year.

(The rest of the year's entries were fairly mundane, implying that life at Ivy Cottage, Landour, went on pretty smoothly. But the rain gods played a trick or two. Although they were fairly generous to begin with, the year ended with a drought, as my mid-December entry indicates: 'Dust covers everything, after nearly two and half months of dry weather. Clouds build up, but disperse.' Always receptive to Nature's unpredictability, I wrote my story *Dust on the Mountain*.)

1995

On the flyleaf of this year's diary are written two maxims: 'Pull your own strings' and 'Act impeccably'. I'm not sure that I did either with much success, but I did at least try. And trying is what it's all about...

January

My book of poems and prayers finally published by Thomson Press, *seven years* after acceptance. Received a copy. Hope it won't be the only one. Splendid illustrations by Suddha. (Shortly afterwards Thomson Press closed down their children's book division and my book vanished too!)

Can thought (consciousness) exist outside the body? Can it, be trained to do so? Can its existence continue after the body has gone? Does it *need* a body? (but without a body it would have nothing to do.)

Of course thoughts can travel. But do they travel of their own volition, or because of the bodily energy that sustains them?

We have the wonders of clairvoyance, of presentiments, and premonitions in dreams. How to account for these?

Our thinking is conditioned by past experience (including the past experience of the human race), and so, as Bergson said: 'We think with only a small part of the past, but it is with our entire past, including the original bent of the soul, that we desire, will, and act.'

'The original bent of the soul...' I accept that man has a soul, or he would be incapable of compassion.

February

We move from mind to matter:

Tried a pizza—seemed to take an hour to travel down my gullet.

Two days later: Swiss cheese pie with Mrs Goel who's Swiss—and more adventures of the digestive tract.

Next day: supper with the Deutschmanns from Australia. Australian pie.

Following day: rest and recovery. Then reverted to good old dal bhaat.

Accompanied N—to Dehra Dun and ended up paying for our lunch. The trouble with rich people is that they never seem to have any money on them. That's how they stay rich, I suppose.

March

Sold A *Crow for All Seasons* to the Children's Film Society for a small sum. They think it will make a good animated film. And so it will. But I'm pretty sure they won't make it. They have forgotten about the story they bought from me five years ago! (Neither film was ever made.)

April

The wind in the pines and deodars hums and moans, but in the chestnut it rustles and chatters and makes cheerful conversation. The horse-chestnut in full leaf is a magnificent sight.

∽

Children down with mumps. I go clown with a viral fever for

two days. Recover and write three articles. Hope for the best. It is not in mortals to *command* success.

∽

Men get their sensual natures from their mothers, their intellectual make-up from their fathers; women, the other way round. (Or so I'm told!)

June

Not many years ago you had to walk for weeks to reach the pilgrim destinations—Badrinath, Gangotri, Kedarnath, Tungnath... Last week, within a few days, I covered them all, as most of them are now accessible by motorable road. I liked some of the smaller places, such as Nandprayag, which are still unspoilt. Otherwise, I'm afraid the *dhaba*-culture of urban India has followed the cars and buses into the mountains and up to the shrines.

July

The deodar (unlike the pine) is a hospitable tree. It allows other things to grow beneath it, and it tolerates growth upon its trunk and branches—moss, ferns, small plants. The tiny young cones are like blossoms on the dark green foliage at this time of the year.

∽

Slipped and cracked my head against the grid of a truck. Blood gushed forth, so I dashed across to Dr Joshi's little clinic and had three stitches and an anti-tetanus shot. Now you know why I don't travel well.

〜

M.C. Beautiful, seductive. 'She walks in beauty like the night...'

August

Endless rain. No sun for a week. But M.C. playful, loving. In good spirits, I wrote a funny story about cricket. I'd find it hard to write a serious story about cricket. The farcical element appeals to me more than the 'nobler' aspects of the game. Uncle Ken made more runs with his pads than with his bat. And out of every ten catches that came his way, he took one!

October

Paid rent in advance for next year; paid school fees to end of this year. Broke, but don't owe a paisa to a soul. Ice cream in town with Raki. Came home to find a couple of cheques waiting for me!

M.C. Quick as a vixen, but makes the chase worthwhile.
    We walk in the wind and the rain. Exhilarating.
        Frantic kisses.
        Time to say goodbye!
        When love is swiftly stolen,
        It hasn't time to die.
    When in love, I'm inspired to write bad verse.

    Teilhard de Chardin said it better:
'Some day, after we have mastered the winds, the waves,

the tides and gravity, we shall harness for God the energies of love. Then for the second time in the history of the world, man will have discovered fire.'

February 1986

Destiny is really the strength of our desires.

∽

Raki back from the village. I'm happy he has made himself popular there, adapted to both worlds, the comparative sophistication of Mussoorie and the simple earthiness of village Bachhanshu in the remoteness of Garhwal. Being able to get on with everyone, rich or poor, old or young, makes life so much easier. Or so I've found! My parents' broken marriage, father's early death, and the difficulties of adapting to my stepfather's home, resulted in my being something of a loner until I was thirty. Now I've become a family person without marrying. Selfish?

∽

Returned to two great comic novels—H. G. Wells's *History of Mr Polly* and George and Weedon Grossmith's *Diary of Nobody*. *Polly* has some marvellous set-pieces, while *Nobody* never fails to make me laugh.

∽

M. C. returns with a spring in the Springtime. The same good nature and sense of humour.

Three things in love the foolish will desire:
Faith, constancy, and passion; but the wise
Only an hour's happiness require
And not to look into uncaring eyes.

(Kenneth Hopkins)

March

Getting Granny's Glasses received a nomination for the Carnegie Medal. *Cricket for the Crocodile* makes friends.

After a cold wet spell, Holi brings warmer days, ladybirds, new friends.

May

So now I'm 52. Time to pare life down to the basics of doing.

a) what I have to do
b) what I want to do

Much prefer the latter.

June

Blood pressure up and down.

Writing for a living: it's a battlefield!

People do ask funny questions. Accosted on the road by a stranger, who proceeds to cross-examine me, starting with: 'Excuse me, are you a good writer?' For once, I'm stumped for an answer.

Muki no better. Bangs my study door, sees me give a start, and says: 'This door makes a lot of noise, doesn't it?'

August

Thousands converge on the town from outlying villages, for local festival. By late evening, scores of drunks staggering about on the road. A few fights, but largely good-natured.

The women dress very attractively and colourfully. But for most of the menfolk, the height of fashion appears to be a new pyjama-suit. But I'm a pyjama person myself. Pyjamas are comfortable, I write better wearing pyjamas!

September

Month began with a cheque that bounced. Refrained from checking my blood pressure.

∽

Monsoon growth at its peak. The ladies' slipper orchids are tailing off, but I noticed all the following wild flowers: balsam (two kinds), commelina, agrnnony, wild geranium (very pretty), sprays of white flowers emanating from the wild ginger, the scarlet fruit of the cobra lily just forming tiny mushrooms set like pearls in a retaining wall; ferns still green, which means more rain to come; escaped dahlias everywhere; wild begonias and much else. The best time of year for wild flowers.

February 1987

Home again, after five days in hospital with bleeding ulcers. Loving care from Prem. Support from Ganesh and others. Nurse Nirmala very caring. I prefer nurses to doctors.

Milk, hateful milk!

After a week, back in hospital. Must have been all that milk. Or maybe Nurse Nirmala!

March

To Delhi for a check-up. Public gardens ablaze with flowers. Felt much better.

'A merry heart does good like a medicine, but a broken spirit dries the bones.'

'He who tenderly brings up his servant from a child, shall have him become his son at the end.'

(Book of Proverbs)

May

Lines for future use:

Lunch (at my convent school) was boiled mutton and overcooked pumpkin, which made death lose some of its sting.

Pictures on the wall are not just something to look at. After a time, they become company.

Another bus accident, and a curious crowd gathered with disaster-inspired speed.

He (Upendra) has a bonfire of a laugh.

(Forgot to use these lines, so here they are!)

May

Ordered a birthday cake, but it failed to arrive. Sometimes I think inertia is the greatest force in the world.

Wrote a ghost story, something I enjoy doing from time to

time, although I must admit that, try as I might, I have yet to encounter a supernatural being. Unless you can count dreams as being supernatural experiences.

August

After the drought, the deluge.

Landslide near the house. It rumbled away all night and I kept getting up to see how close it was getting to us. About twenty feet away. The house is none too stable, badly in need of repairs. In fact, it looks a bit like the Lucknow Residency after the rebels had finished shelling it.

(It did, however, survive the landslide, although the retaining wall above our flat collapsed, filling the sitting-room with rubble.)

November

To Delhi, to receive a generous award from Indian Council for Child Education. Presented to me by the Vice-President of India. Got back to my host's home to discover that the envelope contained another awardee's cheque. He was due to leave for Ahmedabad by train. Rushed to railway station, to find him on the platform studying my cheque which he had just discovered in his pocket. Exchanged cheques. All's well that ends well.

A Delhi Visit

A long day's taxi journey to Delhi. It gets tiring towards the end, but I have always found the road journey interesting and at times quite enchanting—especially the rural scene from outside Dehra Dun, through Roorkee and various small wayside towns, up to Muzzafarnagar and the outskirts of Meerut: the sugar-cane being harvested and taken to the sugar factories (by cart or truck); the fruit on sale everywhere (right now, it's the season for bananas and 'chakotra' lemons); children bathing in small canals; the serenity of mango groves...

Of course there's the other side to all this—the litter that accumulates wherever there are large centres of population; the blaring of horns; loudspeakers here and there. It's all part of the picture. But the picture as a whole is a fascinating one, and the colours can't be matched anywhere else.

Marigolds blaze in the sun. Yes, whole fields of them, for they are much in demand on all sorts of ceremonial occasions: marriages, temple pujas, and garlands for dignitaries—making the humble marigold a good cash crop.

And not so humble after all. For although the rose may still be the queen of flowers, and the jasmine the princess of fragrance, the marigold holds its own through sheer sturdiness, colour and cheerfulness. It is a cheerful flower, no doubt about that—brightening up winter days, often when there is little else in bloom. It doesn't really have a fragrance—simply an acid odour, not to everyone's liking—but it has a wonderful range of colour, from lower yellow to deep orange to golden bronze, especially among the giant varieties in the hills.

Otherwise this is not a great month for flowers, although at the India International Centre (IIC) in Delhi, where I am staying, there is a pretty tree with fragile pink flowers—the Chorisnia speciosa, each bloom having five large pink petals, with long pistula.

Adventures in Reading

1

BEAUTY IN SMALL BOOKS

You don't see them so often now, those tiny books and almanacs—genuine pocketbooks—once so popular with our parents and grandparents; much smaller than the average paperback, often smaller than the palm of the hand. With the advent of coffee-table books, new books keep growing bigger and bigger, rivalling tombstones! And one day, like Alice after drinking from the wrong bottle, they will reach the ceiling and won't have anywhere else to go. The average publisher, who apparently believes that large profits are linked to large books, must look upon these old miniatures with amusement or scorn. They were not meant for a coffee table, true. They were meant for true book-lovers and readers, for they took up very little space—you could slip them into your pocket without any discomfort, either to you or to the pocket.

I have a small collection of these little books, treasured over the years. Foremost is my father's prayer-book and psalter, with his name, 'Aubrey Bond, Lovedale, 1917', inscribed on the inside back cover. Lovedale is a school in the Nilgiri Hills in south India, where, as a young man, he did his teacher's training. He gave it to me soon after I went to a boarding school in Shimla in 1944, and my own name is inscribed on it in his beautiful handwriting.

Another beautiful little prayer-book in my collection is called *The Finger Prayer Book*. Bound in soft leather, it is about the same length and breadth as the average middle finger. Replete with psalms, it is the complete book of common prayer and not an abridgement; a marvel of miniature book production.

Not much larger is a delicate item in calf-leather, *The Humour of Charles Lamb*. It fits into my wallet and often stays there. It has a tiny portrait of the great essayist, followed by some thirty to forty extracts from his essays, such as this favourite of mine: 'Every dead man must take upon himself to be lecturing me with his odious truism, that "Such as he is now, I must shortly be". Not so shortly friend, perhaps as thou imaginest. In the meantime, I am alive. I move about. I am worth twenty of thee. Know thy betters!'

No fatalist, Lamb. He made no compromise with Father Time. He affirmed that in age we must be as glowing and tempestuous as in youth! And yet Lamb is thought to be an old-fashioned writer.

Another favourite among my 'little' books is *The Pocket Trivet, An Anthology for Optimists*, published by *The Morning Post* newspaper in 1932. But what is a trivet? the unenlightened may well ask. Well, it's a stand for a small pot or kettle, fixed securely over a grate. To be *right as a trivet* is to be perfectly right. Just right, like the short sayings in this book, which is further enlivened by a number of charming woodcuts based on the seventeenth century originals; such as the illustration of a moth hovering over a candle flame and below it the legend—'I seeke mine owne hurt.'

But the sayings are mostly of a cheering nature, such as Emerson's 'Hitch your wagon to a star!' or the West Indian proverb: 'Every day no Christmas, an' every day no rainy day.'

My book of trivets is a happy example of much concentrated wisdom being collected in a small space—the beauty separated from the dross. It helps me to forget the dilapidated building in which I live and to look instead, at the ever-changing cloud patterns as seen from my bedroom windows. There is no end to the shapes made by the clouds, or to the stories they set off in my head. We don't have to circle the world in order to find beauty and fulfilment. After all, most of living has to happen in the mind. And, to quote one anonymous sage from my trivet, 'The world is only the size of each man's head.'

2
WRITTEN BY HAND

Amongst the current fraternity of writers, I must be that very rare person—an author who actually writes by hand!

Soon after the invention of the typewriter, most editors and publishers understandably refused to look at any mansucript that was handwritten. A decade or two earlier, when Dickens and Balzac had submitted their hefty manuscrips in longhand, no one had raised any objection. Had their handwriting been awful, their manuscripts would still have been read. Fortunately for all concerned, most writers, famous or obscure, took pains over their handwriting. For some, it was an art in itself, and many of those early manuscripts are a pleasure to look at and read.

And it wasn't only authors who wrote with an elegant hand. Parents and grandparents of most of us had distinctive styles of their own. I still have my father's last letter, written to me when I was at boarding school in Shimla some fifty years ago. He used large, beautifully formed letters, and his thoughts seemed to have the same flow and clarity as his handwriting.

In his letter he advises me (then a nine-year-old) about my own handwriting; 'I wanted to write before about your writing. Ruskin...sometimes I get letters from you in very small writing, as if you wanted to squeeze everything into one sheet of letter paper. It is not good for you or for your eyes, to get into the habit of writing too small... Try and form a larger style of handwriting—use more paper if necessary!'

I did my best to follow his advice, and I'm glad to report that after nearly forty years of the writing life, most people can still read my handwriting!

Word-processors are all the rage now, and I have no objection to these mechanical aids any more than I have to my old Olympia typewriter, made in 1956 and still going strong. Although I do all my writing in longhand, I follow the conventions by typing a second draft. But I would not enjoy my writing if I had to do it straight on to a machine. It isn't just the pleasure of writing longhand. I like taking my notebooks and writing-pads to odd places. This particular essay is being written on the steps of my small cottage facing Pari Tibba (Fairy Hill). Part of the reason for sitting here is that there is a new postman on this route, and I don't want him to miss me.

For a freelance writer, the postman is almost as important as a publisher. I could, of course, sit here doing nothing, but as I have pencil and paper with me, and feel like using them, I shall write until the postman comes and maybe after he has gone, too! There is really no way in which I could set up a word-processor on these steps.

There are a number of favourite places where I do my writing. One is under the chestnut tree on the slope above the cottage. Word-processors were not designed keeping mountain slopes in mind. But armed with a pen (or pencil) and paper, I can lie on the grass and write for hours. On one occasion, last month, I did take my typewriter into the garden, and I am still trying to extricate an acorn from under the keys, while the roller seems permanently stained yellow with some fine pollen-dust from the deodar trees.

My friends keep telling me about all the wonderful things I can do with a word-processor, but they haven't got around to finding me one that I can take to bed, for that is another place where I do much of my writing—especially on cold winter nights, when it is impossible to keep the cottage warm.

While the wind howls outside, and snow piles up on the window-sill, I am warm under my quilt, writing pad on my knees, ballpoint pen at the ready. And if, next day, the weather is warm and sunny, these simple aids will accompany me on a long walk, ready for instant use should I wish to record an incident, a prospect, a conversation, or simply a train of thought.

When I think of the great eighteenth and nineteenth century writers, scratching away with their quill pens, filling hundreds of pages every month, I am amazed to find that their handwriting did not deteriorate into the sort of hieroglyphics that often make up the average doctor's prescription today. They knew they had to write legibly, if only for the sake of the typesetters.

Both Dickens and Thackeray had good, clear, flourishing styles. (Thackeray was a clever illustrator, too.) Somerset Maugham had an upright, legible hand. Churchill's neat handwriting never wavered, even when he was under stress. I like the bold, clear, straighforward hand of Abraham Lincoln; it mirrors the man. Mahatma Gandhi, another great soul who fell to the assassin's bullet, had many similarities of both handwriting and outlook.

Not everyone had a beautiful hand. King Henry VIII had an untidy scrawl, but then, he was not a man of much refinement. Guy Fawkes, who tried to blow up the British Parliament, had a very shaky hand. With such a quiver, no wonder he failed in his attempt! Hitler's signature is ugly, as you would expect. And Napoleon's doesn't seem to know where to stop; how much like the man!

I think my father was right when he said handwriting was often the key to a man's character, and that large well-formed letters went with an uncluttered mind. Florence Nightingale had a lovely handwriting, the hand of a caring person. And there were many like her, amongst our forebears.

3
WORDS AND PICTURES

When I was a small boy, no Christmas was really complete unless my Christmas stocking contained several recent issues of my favourite comic paper. If today my friends complain that I am too voracious a reader of books, they have only these comics to blame; for they were the origin, if not of my tastes in reading, then certainly of the reading habit itself.

I like to think that my conversion to comics began at the age of five, with a comic strip on the children's page of *The Statesman*. In the late 1930s, Benji, whose head later appeared only on the Benji League badge, had a strip to himself; I don't remember his adventures very clearly, but every day (or was it once a week?) I would cut out the Benji strip and paste it into a scrapbook. Two years later this scrapbook, bursting with the adventures of Benji, accompanied me to boarding school, where, of course, it passed through several hands before finally passing into limbo.

Of course comics did not form the only reading matter that found its way into my Christmas stocking. Before 1 was eight, I had read *Peter Pan, Alice,* and most of *Mr Midshipman Easy;* but I had also consumed thousands of comic-papers which were, after all, slim affairs and mostly pictorial, 'certain little penny books radiant with gold and rich with bad pictures', as Leigh Hunt described the children's papers of his own time.

But though they were mostly pictorial, comics in those days did have a fair amount of reading matter, too. The *Hostspur, Wizard, Magnet* (a victim of the Second World War) and *Champion* contained stories woven round certain popular characters. In *Champion*, which I read regularly right through my prep school years, there was Rockfist Rogan, Royal Air Force (R.A.F.), a pugilist who managed to combine boxing with bombing, and Fireworks Flynn, a footballer who always scored the winning goal in the last two minutes of play

Billy Bunter has, of course, become one of the immortals—almost a subject for literary and social historians. Quite recently, *The Times Literary Supplement* devoted its first two pages to an analysis of the Bunter stories. Eminent lawyers and doctors still look back nostalgically to the arrival of the weekly *Magnet;* they are now the principal customers for the special souvenir edition of the first issue of the *Magnet,* recently reprinted in facsimile. Bunter, 'forever young', has become a folk-hero. He is seen on stage, screen and television, and is even quoted in the House of Commons.

From this, I take courage. My only regret is that I did not preserve my own early comics—not because of any bibliophilic value which they might possess today, but because of my sentimental regard for early influences in art and literature.

The first venture in children's publishing, in 1774 was a comic of sorts. In that year, John Newberry brought out:

> According to Act of Parliament (neatly bound and gilt):
> A Little Pretty Pocket-Book, intended for the Instruction
> and Amusement of Little Master Tommy and Pretty
> Miss Polly, with an agreeable Letter to read from Jack
> the Giant-Killer...

The book contained pictures, rhymes and games. Newberry's

characters and imaginary authors included Woglog the Giant, Tommy Trip, Giles Gingerbread, Nurse Truelove, Peregrine Puzzlebrains, Primrose Prettyface, and many others with names similar to those found in the comic-papers of our own century.

Newberry was also the originator of the 'Amazing Free Offer', so much a part of American comics. At the beginning of 1755, he had this to offer:

Nurse Truelove's New Year Gift, or the Book of Books for children, adorned with cuts and designed as a present for every little boy who would become a great man and ride upon a fine horse; and to every little girl who would become a great woman and ride in a Lord Mayor's gilt coach. Printed for the author, who has ordered these books to be given gratis to all little boys in St. Paul's churchyard, they paying for the binding, which is only two pence each book.

Many of today's comics are crude and, like many television serials violent in their appeal. But I did not know American comics until I was twelve, and by then I had become quite discriminating. Superman, Bulletman, Batman, Green Lantern, and other superheroes all left me cold. I had, by then, passed into the world of real books but the weakness for the comic-strip remains. I no longer receive comics in my Christmas stocking; but I do place a few in the stockings of Gautam and Siddharth. And, needless to say, I read them right through beforehand.

The Postman Knocks

As a freelance writer, most of my adult life has revolved around the coming of the postman. 'A cheque in the mail,' is something that every struggling writer looks forward to. It might, of course, arrive by courier, or it might not come at all. But for the most part, the acceptances and rejections of my writing life, along with editorial correspondence, readers' letters, page proofs and author's copies—how welcome they are!—come through the post.

The postman has always played a very real and important part in my life, and continues to do so. He climbs my twenty-one steps every afternoon, knocks loudly on my door—three raps, so that I know it's him and not some inquisitive tourist—and gives me my registered mail or speed-post with a smile and a bit of local gossip. The gossip is important. I like to know what's happening in the bazaar—who's getting married, who's standing for election, who ran away with the headmaster's wife, and whose funeral procession is passing by. He deserves a bonus for this sort of information.

The courier boy, by contrast, shouts to me from the road below and I have to go down to him. He's mortally afraid of dogs and there are three in the building. My postman isn't bothered by dogs. He comes in all weathers, and he comes on foot except when someone gives him a lift. He turns up when it's snowing, or when it's raining cats and dogs, or when there's a heat wave, and he's quite philosophical about it all. He meets all kinds of people. He has seen joy and sorrow in the homes he visits. He knows something about life. If he wasn't a philosopher to begin with, he will certainly be one by the time he retires.

Of course, not all postmen are paragons of virtue. A few years ago, we had a postman who never got further than the country liquor shop in the bazaar. The mail would pile up there for days, until he sobered up and condescended to deliver it. In due course he was banished to another route, where there were no liquor shops.

We take the postman for granted today, but there was a time, over a hundred years ago, when the carrying of the mails was a hazardous venture, and the mail-runner, or hirkara as he was called, had to be armed with sword or spear. Letters were carried in leather wallets on the backs of runners, who were changed at stages of eight miles. At night, the runners were accompanied by torch-bearers—in wilder parts, by drummers called *dug-dugi wallas*—to frighten away wild animals.

The tiger population was considerable at the time, and tigers were a real threat to travellers or anyone who ventured far from their town or village. Mail-runners often fell victim to man-eating tigers. The mail-runners (most of them tribals) were armed with bows and arrows, but these were seldom effective.

In the Hazaribagh district (through which the mail had to be carried, on its way from Calcutta to Allahabad) there appears to have been a concentration of man-eating tigers. There were four passes through this district, and the tigers had them well covered. Williamson, writing in 1810, tells us that the passes were so infested with tigers that the roads were almost impassable. 'Day after day, for nearly a fortnight, some of the dak people were carried off at one or other of these passes.'

In spite of these hazards, a letter sent by dak runner used to take twelve days to reach Meerut from Calcutta. It takes about the same time today, unless you use speed-post.

At up country stations the collector of Land Revenue was the Postmaster. He was given a small postal establishment, consisting of *a munshi, a matsaddi* or sorter, and thirty or for, runners whose pay, in 1804, was five rupees a month. The maintenance of the dak cost the government (i.e., the East India Company) twenty-five rupees a month for each stage of eight miles. Postage stamps were introduced in 1854.

My father was an enthusastic philatelist, and when I was a small boy I could sit and watch him pore over his stamp collection, which included several early and valuable Indian issues. He would grumble at the very dark and smudgy postmarks which obliterated most of Queen Victoria's profile from the stamps. This was due to the composition of the ink used for cancelling the earlier stamps. It was composed of two parts lamp-black, four parts linseed oil and three and a half of vinegar.

Letter-distributing peons, or postmen, were always smartly turned out: 'A red turban, a light green chapkan, a small leather belt over the breast and right shoulder, with a chaprass attached showing the peon's number and having the words "Post Office Peon" in English and in two vernaculars, and a bell suspended by a leather strap from the left shoulder.'

Today's postmen are more casual in their attire, although I believe they are still entitled to uniforms. The general public doesn't care how they are dressed, as long as they turn up with those letters containing rakhis or money orders from soldiers, peons and husbands. This is where the postman still scores over the fax and email.

To return to our mail-runners, they were eventually replaced by the dak-ghari, the equivalent of the English 'coach and pair'—which gradually established itself throughout the country.

A survivor into the 1940s, my great-aunt Lillian recalled that in the late nineteenth century, before the coming of the railway, the only way of getting to Dehra Dun was by the *dak-ghari* or Night Mail. Dak-ghari ponies were difficult animals, she told me—'always attempting to turn around and get into the carriage with the passengers!' But once they started there was no stopping them. It was a gallop all the way to the first stage, where the ponies were changed to the accompaniment of a bugle blown by the coachman, in true Dickensian fashion.

The journey through the Siwaliks really began—as it still does—through the Mohand Pass. The ascent starts with a gradual gradient which increases as the road becomes more steep and winding. At this stage of the journey, drums were beaten (if it was day) and torches lit (if it was night) because sometimes wild elephants resented the approach of the *dak-ghari* and, trumpeting a challenge, would throw the ponies into confusion and panic, and send them racing back to the plains.

After 1900, great-aunt Lillian used the train. But the main bus from Saharanpur to Mussoorie still uses the old route through the Siwaliks. And if you are lucky, you may see a herd of wild elephants crossing the road on its way to the Ganga.

And even today, in remote parts of the country, in isolated hill areas where there are no motorable roads, the mail is carried on foot, the postman often covering five or six miles every day. He never runs, true, and be might sometimes stop for a glass of tea and a game of cards en-route, but he is a reminder of those early pioneers of the postal system, the mail-runners of India.

$\backsim$

Let me not cavil at my unexpected visitors. Sometimes they turn out to be very nice people—like the gentleman from Pune who brought me a bottle of whisky and then sat down and drank most of it himself.

George and Ranji

When I heard that my cousin George had again escaped from the mental hospital in a neighbouring town, I knew it wouldn't be long before he turned up at my doorstep. It usually happens at the approach of the cricket season. No problem, I thought. I'll just bundle him into a train and take him back to the hospital.

Cousin George had been there, off and on, for a few years. He wasn't the violent type and was given a certain amount of freedom—with the result that he occasionally wandered off by himself, sometimes, to try and take in a Test match. You see, George did not suffer from the delusion that he was Napoleon or Ghengis Khan, he was convinced that he was the great Ranji, Prince of Cricketers, and that he had just been selected to captain India—quite forgetting that Ranji had actually played for England!

So when George turned up on my front step I wan't surprised to find him carrying a cricket bat in one hand and a protective box in the other.

'Aren't you ready?' he asked. 'The match starts at 11.'

'There's plenty of time,' I said, recalling that the train left at 11.15. 'Why don't you come in and relax while I get ready?'

George sat down and asked for a glass of beer. I brought him one and he promptly emptied it over a pot of ferns.

'They look thirsty,' he said. I dressed hurriedly, anxious to get moving before he started practising his latest cuts on my cutglass decanter. Then, arm in arm, we walked to the gate and hailed an auto rickshaw.

'Railway station,' I whispered to the driver.

'Ferozeshah Kotla,' said George in rising tones, naming Delhi's famous cricket ground. No matter. I thought, I'll straighten out the driver as we go along, I bundled George into the rickshaw and we were soon heading in the direction of the Kotla.

'Railway station,' I said again, in tones that could not be denied.

'Kotla,' said cousin George, just as firmly.

The scooter driver kept right on course for the cricket ground. Apparently George had made a better impression on him.

'Look,' I said, tapping the driver on the shoulder. 'This is my cousin and he's not quite right in the head. He's just escaped from a mental asylum and if I'm to get him back there tonight, we must catch the 11.15 train.'

The scooter driver slowed down and looked from cousin George to me and back again. George gave him a winning smile and looking in my direction, tapped his forehead significantly. The driver nodded in sympathy and kept straight on for the Kotla.

Well, I've always believed that the dividing line between

sanity and insanity is a very thin one, but I had never realised it was quite so thin—too thin for my own comfort! Who was crazy—George, me or the driver?

We had almost reached the Kotla and I had no intention of watching over cousin George through a whole day's play. He gets excited at cricket matches—which is strange considering how dull they can be. On one occasion, he broke through the barriers and walked up to the wicket with his bat, determined to bat at No. 3 (Ranji's favourite position, apparently) and assaulted an umpire who tried to escort him from the ground. On another occasion he streaked across the ground, wearing nothing but his protective box.

But it was I who confirmed the driver's worst fears by jumping off the rickshaw as it slowed down, and making my getaway. I've never been able to discover if cousin George had any money with him, or if the rickshaw driver got paid. Rickshaw drivers are inclined at times to be violent, but then so are inmates of mental hospitals. Anyway, George seems to have no memory of the incident.

Three days later, I received a word from the hospital that he had returned of his own accord, boasting that he had hit a century, so presumably, he had participated in the match in some form or another.

All's well that ends well, or so I like to think. Cousin George was not usually a violent man, but I have a funny feeling about the rickshaw driver. I never saw him again in Delhi, and unless he had moved elsewhere, I'm afraid his disappearance might well be connected with cousin George's rickshaw ride. After all, the Jamuna is very near the Kotla.

My Failed Omelettes—and Other Disasters

In nearly fifty years of writing for a living, I have never succeeded in writing a bestseller. And now I know why. I can't cook.

Had I been able to do so, I could have turned out a few of those sumptuous-looking cookery books that brighten up the bookstore windows before being snapped up by folk who can't cook either.

As it is, if I were forced to write a cook book, it would probably be called *Fifty Different Ways of Boiling an Egg*, and other disasters.

I used to think that boiling an egg would be a simple undertaking. But when I came to live at 7,000 ft in the Himalayan foothills, I found that just getting the water to boil was something of an achievement. I don't know if it's the altitude or the density of the water, but it just won't come to the boil in time for breakfast. As a result my eggs are only half-boiled. 'Never mind,' I tell everyone; 'half-boiled eggs are more nutritious than full-boiled eggs.'

'Why boil them at all?' asks my five-year-old grandson, Gautam, who is my Mr Dick, always offering good advice. 'Raw eggs are probably healthier.'

'Just you wait and see,' I told him. 'I'll make you a cheese omelette you'll never forget.' And I did. It was a bit messy, as I was over-generous with the tomatoes, but I thought it tasted rather good. Gautam, however, pushed his plate away, saying, 'You forgot to put in the egg.'

101 Failed Omelettes might well be the title of my bestseller.

I love watching other people cook–a habit that I acquired at a young age, when I would watch my Granny at work in the kitchen, turning out delicious curries, koftas and custards. I would try helping her, but she soon put a stop to my feeble contributions. On one occasion she asked me to add a cup of spices to a large curry dish she was preparing, and absent-mindedly I added a cup of sugar. The result—a very sweet curry! Another invention of mine.

I was better at remembering Granny's kitchen proverbs. Here are some of them:

'There is skill in all things, even in making porridge.'

'Dry bread at home is better then curried prawns abroad.'

'Eating and drinking should not keep men from thinking.'

'Better a small fish than an empty dish.'

And her favourite maxim, with which she reprimanded me whenever I showed signs of gluttony: 'Don't let your tongue cut your throat.'

And as for making porridge, it's certainly no simple matter.

I made one or two attempts, but it always came out lumpy. 'What's this?' asked Gautam suspiciously, when I offered him some.

'Porridge!' I said enthusiastically. 'It's eaten by those brave Scottish Highlanders who were always fighting the English!'

'And did they win?' he asked.

'Well—er—not usually But they were outnumbered!'

He looked doubtfully at the porridge. 'Some other time,' he said.

So why not take the advice of Thoreau and try to simplify life? Simplify, simplify! Or simply sandwiches...

These shouldn't be too difficult, I decided. After all, they are basically bread and butter. But have you tried cutting bread into thin slices? Don't. It's highly dangerous. If you're a pianist, you could be putting your career at great risk.

You must get your bread ready sliced. Butter it generously. Now add your fillings. Cheese, tomato, lettuce, cucumber, whatever. Gosh, I was really going places! Slap another slice of buttered bread over this mouth-watering assemblage. Now cut in two. Result: Everything spills out at the sides and on to the tablecloth.

'Now look what you've gone and done,' says Gautam, in his best Oliver Hardy manner.

'Never mind,' I tell him. 'Practice makes perfect!'

And one of these days you're going to find *Bond's Book of Better Sandwiches* up there on the bestseller lists.